Speak

Table of Contents

1. CYRUS FINCH .... Page 3
2. DR. CREED .... Page 11
3. CYRUS FINCH .... Page 14
4. DR. CREED .... Page 20
5. CYRUS FINCH .... Page 24
6. DR. CREED .... Page 29
7. CYRUS FINCH .... Page 35
8. DR. CREED .... Page 40
9. CYRUS FINCH .... Page 44
10. DR. CREED .... Page 48
11. CYRUS FINCH .... Page 51
12. DR. CREED .... Page 54
13. CYRUS FINCH .... Page 57
14. DR. CREED .... Page 62
15. CYRUS FINCH .... Page 66
16. DR. CREED .... Page 74
17. CYRUS FINCH .... Page 79
18. DR. CREED .... Page 84
19. CYRUS FINCH .... Page 89
20. DR. CREED .... Page 95
21. CYRUS FINCH .... Page 102
22. DR. CREED .... Page 109
23. CYRUS FINCH .... Page 112
24. DR. CREED .... Page 117
25. CYRUS FINCH .... Page 123
26. DR. CREED .... Page 127
27. CYRUS FINCH .... Page 130
28. DR. CREED .... Page 132
29. CYRUS FINCH .... Page 136
30. DR. CREED .... Page 140
31. CYRUS FINCH .... Page 143
32. DR. CREED .... Page 145
33. CYRUS FINCH .... Page 151
34. DR. CREED .... Page 154
35. Teaser   .... Page 157

Cyrus Finch

I opened my eyes to a dreamy world, taking in the early morning suburban streets from a unique vantage point. I was no longer Cyrus Finch, the teenage boy burdened by life's complexities. In this surreal vision, I saw the world through the eyes of a dog, and the world was filled with wonder.

As the sun timidly ascended, I took off, paws pounding the pavement, driven by the simple desire to explore. I would stop intermittently, captivated by intriguing scents that beckoned my attention. Life was different as a dog, a simpler existence, free from the burdens of human consciousness.

Yet, even in this dream, my thoughts betrayed my canine form. I contemplated my family, a topic that had dominated my waking hours. The words formed in my mind, both a confession and a question.

"My name is Cyrus Finch, and this is the story of how I killed my family," I whispered in the dream, the weight of those words still evident even in my altered state. "In hindsight, would I follow that same path knowing I'd lose everybody?"

With a sense of nostalgia, my dream self-rounded a corner, heading down an unfamiliar street. There, the dream took an intriguing twist. I found myself embracing my family, or rather, the illusion of my family.

They appeared in the dream like characters in a storybook. My mother, Mrs. Finch, was still a loving but strict figure, her vibrant red hair and keen green eyes radiating warmth. My father, Mr. Finch, remained a burly man with a thick Irish accent. Erin, my little sister, confined to a wheelchair, was as lighthearted as ever, absorbed in a book. And Chase, our German shepherd, was the loyal companion who graced our lives.

In this dream, I watched them from my dog's perspective, a seemingly inconsequential observer. Mom's words and dad's newspaper made it all feel real, even though I knew it was just a mirage of my family. The scent of eggs and bacon filled the air, creating an illusion of breakfast being served.

But my dream took another unexpected turn. I began to sense that I wasn't merely observing. I felt a connection to Chase, a connection that transcended the boundaries of the dream. The dog's world became mine, and I could see it through his eyes. His actions felt real and vivid, as if I were truly inside his furry form.

Then, the dream allowed me to glimpse the morning ritual in my family's home. It felt like I was living within them, experiencing their lives, almost as if I were chasing the elusive memories of a happier time.

In the dream, my family interactions unfolded as if I were one with Chase, and that peculiar connection lingered. I watched my mother reprimanding Chase to keep the house clean, heard my sister's endearing complaint, and even my father's humorous response about the source of Chase's issues. I was part of it all, a silent participant in the domesticity of my family.

The dream seamlessly transitioned from these ordinary moments into a less tangible, darker reality. My laptop, my solitary haven, was gone, replaced by a newfound curiosity. An email notification grabbed my attention, and I couldn't resist clicking on it. The subject line read, "EVERYTHING TO KNOW ABOUT INUGAMI."

As I read through the email, a sense of intrigue overcame me. The forbidden rituals, the outlawed practices, and the fervent beliefs behind the enigmatic concept of Inugami fascinated my dream self. It was as if I were on the cusp of a hidden world, ready to explore its mysteries.

Reality and the dream blurred together, and I felt an inexplicable sense of unity with the dream's embodiment of my family. It was as though I could see through their eyes, just as I had seen through Chase's.

With the transition from dream to reality, my consciousness awakened. The line between dream and reality remained hazy, but one thing was clear: my connection to my dog, Chase, might have extended beyond mere dreams. In the waking world, I was Cyrus Finch, but this experience had left me with the lingering notion that I could peer into the world through the eyes of my faithful companion, Chase.

The dream, though fleeting, had left an indelible mark on my mind. The peculiar connection I'd experienced between Chase's eyes and my own lingered as I slowly emerged from the haze of early morning consciousness. My room materialized around me, adorned with anime and superhero posters that had always defined my space.

Yet, it was the black eye, a battle scar from yesterday's confrontation with bullies, that caught my attention. It was as if my reflection in the mirror belonged to someone else, a distant figure gazing back at me.

My laptop beckoned, and I instinctively reached for it. A compulsion I couldn't resist drove me to check my emails, to delve deeper into the enigmatic Inugami that had piqued my interest in the dream. It was as though the dream world's curtain had been lifted, urging me to explore the mysteries it had hinted at.

Mom's voice disrupted my reverie, calling me to breakfast. Her words grounded me, pulling me away from the dream's allure. I sighed, reluctantly putting aside the email, though my thoughts still revolved around it.

It was time to face the day, to confront the world outside. Reluctantly, I closed my laptop, but the dream's lingering presence was impossible to ignore. A nagging thought persisted—could the connection I'd experienced with Chase in that dream hold any truth?

Breakfast was a familiar affair in our cozy kitchen, and the exchange between Dad and Mom, their affectionate bickering, played out just as it had in my dream. I took my usual seat at the table, and the ordinary routine resumed, but something felt different, as if I'd glimpsed a parallel reality in my dream.

Erin, my intellectually gifted sister, was engrossed in the pages of "Harry Potter and the Chamber of Secrets." Her innocence and bright spirit provided a stark contrast to the turmoil that had recently engulfed my life.

Yet, beneath the surface of our mundane morning, a gnawing realization lingered. The dark specter of cancer, which my dream had briefly touched upon, cast a long shadow over our lives. It had taken my loyal companion, Chase, and it had the power to threaten the lives of my family.

The insidious grip of cancer had left my family vulnerable, and their vulnerability weighed heavily on my heart. I could see it in Erin's eyes, hidden behind her youthful curiosity, and in Mom and Dad's weary gazes. I longed to shield them from the harsh reality my dream had hinted at.

I looked at my family members, and I couldn't help but wonder if the strange connection between Chase and me in the dream was merely a fantasy or a glimpse into something deeper. A faint, persistent thought hovered in my mind—a possibility that I might find a way to save my faithful companion, to confront the curse of disease that had befallen him.

But for now, I kept my thoughts to myself, eating my breakfast with a heavy heart and carrying the weight of my family's love, along with my secret desire to change their fate. The ordinary morning continued, but the resolve to uncover the truth of the dream and the potential link between Chase and me remained steadfast within me.

I finished my breakfast, the taste of scrambled eggs and crispy bacon offering a fleeting comfort in the midst of my turbulent life. Determined to face another challenging day at school, I left the kitchen quietly, my mind already preparing for the expected taunts and jeers from my classmates.

Walking down the school bus lane, I kept my gaze fixed on the ground, hoping for a peaceful ride. Finding an empty seat in the middle of the bus, I settled in, but peace remained elusive. A painful flick to the back of my ear made me wince, and despite my father's advice, I couldn't resist turning around.

A harsh slap on the back of my neck propelled me forward, igniting my anger. I faced the culprits – Tyrell and Miguel, two of the school's mediocre bullies. Their laughter echoed as the bus continued its route.

Then, a new girl, Alice, stepped on. With her mysterious aura, brunette hair, and eyes bearing scars of a life touched by war, she approached me. "Can I join you?" she asked, and I, dumbstruck, could only nod.

As she sat beside me, Tyrell and Miguel attempted another flick, but Alice's glare silenced the entire bus. Her icy tone pierced the air as she warned the bullies. They nervously retreated into their own conversation, avoiding Alice's attention.

Turning to me with a warm smile, she extended her hand. "Hi, my name is Alice. I just moved here." I nervously took her hand and introduced myself as Cyrus.

"Why do you let them do that to you?" she questioned, her gaze penetrating mine. I hesitated before admitting, "My father said that if I react, they'll keep doing it. I just want them to stop."

"Then make them," Alice urged, her tone unwavering.

...

Walking down the school hallway with Alice by my side, a heavy silence lingered between us. Eventually, she broke it, thanking me for showing her around. I responded with a bored expression, stating that there was no need to thank me.

Curiosity sparkled in her eyes as she asked if everything was a transaction for me. I contemplated before responding, "Everything in this world is a transaction. From this conversation to your wants and needs."

She studied me, questioning what she wanted. "And what do I want, Cyrus?"

I considered her words. "You want excitement, a cause to fight for. So, you're trying to befriend the kid who gets bullied."

Alice's eyes drifted away, and a silence followed before she admitted, "Perhaps you're right. I don't have enough information to form my own opinion yet."

Reaching the restroom, we came to a halt. Alice surprised me with an awkward hug before heading to her last period, leaving me to ponder our intriguing exchange and the budding connection with the enigmatic newcomer.

I walked into the school bathroom, lost in thought, oblivious to the taunts of Tyrell and Miguel echoing from the hallway. The events of the morning still consumed my mind, particularly the enigmatic encounter with Alice and her words of encouragement.

As I ventured deeper into the bathroom, I remained distanced from my surroundings. My detachment left me vulnerable, and it didn't take long before a powerful fist struck me, sending me tumbling to the floor. Stunned, I saw black spots and blinked rapidly, attempting to regain my senses while clutching my throbbing head.

Amidst the chaos, a voice cut through the haze. "Pick him up," it ordered. I struggled to focus and turned my gaze toward the source. Tyrell stood on my left, tugging on my arm, while Miguel examined his knuckles after delivering the punch. In the middle of it all, Josh leaned casually against a sink.

I rose to my feet, my anger growing, and locked eyes with Josh, a bitter, resentful glare etched on my face. He wasted no time in taunting me. "I heard you had a 'girl' stand up for you today," he sneered, glancing at Miguel. "Grab his other arm."

In the distance, an echo of a previous conversation played in my mind. I recalled my admission to Alice, "I just want them to stop," and her response, "Then make them."

Fueled by a mix of rage and desperation, I yanked my arm from Miguel's grasp, a sharp pain shooting through my shoulder. I let out a scream but pressed forward, attempting to lunge at Josh. However, Miguel and Tyrell reacted swiftly, overpowering me and forcing me back to the ground.

Josh advanced with a cruel smile; his intention clear. "He looks thirsty. Put his head in the toilet so he can get refreshed."

My struggles intensified, and I found myself dragged closer to the toilet, trapped in a nightmarish encounter with my tormentors.

Amid the horrifying sounds of my screams, gasps for air, and a chorus of curses, the climax of this torment came in the unmistakable sound of a toilet flushing, a chilling and dark resolution to the harrowing ordeal I endured.
...

A week had passed since the traumatic incident in the school bathroom. I found myself seated in Dr. Creed's office as the evening sun cast long shadows in the dimly lit room. Dr. Creed, his demeanor composed, carefully examined the visible bruises that marred my body, all the while making notations in his book.

He looked up from his notes and offered a gentle welcome, "Welcome back to school."

I squirmed in the chair, the physical and emotional wounds still fresh. "So... how are you doing?" I inquired, striving to maintain a facade of composure.

After a moment's pause, Dr. Creed responded, "I'm well. How are you?"

I hesitated, weighing how much I should divulge. "I'm good," I replied, choosing not to burden him with the depth of my suffering.

Dr. Creed, perceptive as ever, didn't press further. "I heard about the... incident. Would you like to talk about it?"

The perspective shifted, plunging me back into the memory of that horrifying moment when my face was thrust into the toilet bowl, subjecting me to a nightmarish suffocation. I was yanked up for a brief gasp of air, only to be submerged again.

Back in Dr. Creed's office, I shook my head in response to his inquiry. "Nope."

With gentle persistence, Dr. Creed suggested, "Perhaps you should."

I remained silent, unable to escape the relentless replay of that bathroom ordeal in my mind.

Dr. Creed altered his approach. "How's Chase?"

A whirlwind of emotions passed across my face, each emotion a painful reminder of the torment I was enduring.

A week ago, in my modest backyard, the same as the house, the grass was a muddy green, with scattered rocks dotting the landscape. Still bearing the visible bruises from my ordeal, I stepped out of the back door.

"Chase! Where are you?" I called out, the anxiety evident in my voice as I scoured the field. At last, I spotted Chase, his body limp and barely breathing. Panic surged through me as I rushed to his side, my hands trembling with fear.

Desperation filled my voice as I tried to comfort Chase, "Chase, buddy, you're going to be okay."

Tears welled in my eyes as I returned to the present and answered Dr. Creed, "He's not doing well."

Dr. Creed looked at me with sympathy and asked, "Is there anything I can do?"

My gaze met his, a deep sorrow in my eyes. "Can you cure cancer?"

A dry laugh escaped Dr. Creed. "Some believe cancer to have been created by dark, evil magic, beyond the reach of any known beings."

I nodded in understanding. "I might've found a way to save him."

My mind shifted back to my frantic digging in the backyard, my tears blending with the soil as I cried out to myself, "Don't worry, Chase, I'm going to save you."

I continued to dig until the ditch was deep enough, burying Chase up to his neck. His whimpers filled the air as I placed him inside, my hands offering a gentle caress to his head before covering the hole, leaving only his head exposed.

"I love you, boy," I whispered to him as I reluctantly abandoned my best friend, his whimpers echoing in the background.

The final school bell rang, marking the end of another day and bringing me back to reality. I stood up, collected my belongings, and gazed at Dr. Creed.

"I don't know too much about it yet," I admitted, my voice heavy with the weight of the past week. "But I will let you know what I find out."

I walked toward the door, my mind still weighed down by the recent events.

"See you later, doc," I said, offering a small, appreciative nod before stepping out of the office and into the uncertain future that awaited me.

Dr CREED

The soft glow of evening filtered through the window, casting long shadows that stretched like phantom fingers across the room. In the wake of Cyrus Finch's departure from my office, I found myself reflecting on the dangerous path I had set him upon. His final words lingered in the air, a haunting reminder of the secrets and manipulations that bound us together, an intricate tapestry of deception that had the power to shape the fate of the world.

Cyrus, an enigma of resilience and determination, harbored a strength that transcended his years. It was a strength that had grown within him, subtly nurtured and cultivated, driven by the unwavering love for his faithful companion, Chase. The boy remained blissfully unaware of the deeper truths, a shadowy labyrinth of my past and the calamitous blunder that I was determined to rectify.

Once, I had not been the unassuming Dr. Creed, but rather Samuel Creed, a name that had struck fear and reverence into the hearts of those who knew of my existence. Concealed beneath the cloak of Samuel Creed was a Nogitsune, a being capable of shape-shifting and orchestrating the symphony of human minds, an entity that reveled in the chaos of deception.

In a different life, I had harnessed these formidable abilities to further my ambitions, to amass knowledge, and to seize dominion over power. Yet, in doing so, I had unwittingly set into motion the catastrophic series of events that had led to my ultimate folly.

The transformation from Samuel Creed, the Nogitsune wielding boundless power, to Dr. Creed, the unassuming physician, had been a conscious choice driven by an insatiable desire for redemption. However, the treacherous line between mentorship and manipulation had been transgressed, as I sought salvation and the means to set right the irreversible destruction I had sown.

The truth of my previous existence, my hubris, and the relentless repercussions of my actions weighed heavily upon me. I recollected the ill-fated encounter with Peter, an otherworldly entity of malevolence, a creature that I had believed I could bend to my will. It had been my audacious attempt to tamper with the delicate balance between life and death that had succeeded in reviving Peter, not as a human, but as something infinitely more sinister.

Peter, reborn with nefarious powers, had spiraled into a malevolent force that I was woefully unequipped to control. He had turned on me, exploiting the newfound extent of his capabilities to sew discord and unleash anarchy. The consequences of my actions had been devastating, and I shouldered the weight of those mistakes with a heavy heart.

Cyrus Finch had emerged as the critical component in stemming the tide of the relentless threat I had inadvertently released upon the world. The menace had its origins in my arrogance and audacity, and Cyrus had been cultivated in the shadows, expertly shaped to become a guardian, a sentinel of the world. The moral complexity of my actions gnawed at my conscience, for I had manipulated him without his awareness or consent, sculpting him into a weapon of salvation.

The room was bathed in the haunting dance of shadows that mirrored the intricacies of the web I had woven around Cyrus. The boundaries between guidance and manipulation had blurred, and the choices I had made to shield the world from the malevolence of my creation were far from straightforward. The fate of the world rested precariously on Cyrus's shoulders, and the path to redemption was fraught with uncertainty.

Cyrus Finch, unwittingly manipulated, was the pawn in my quest for salvation, the weapon honed through secrecy and subterfuge. Yet, as I observed him leave my office, I couldn't escape the disquieting truth that had guided my choices from the inception of our entwined destinies.

Cyrus Finch was a sociopath.

This revelation, a truth uncovered long ago, had been the impetus for his recruitment into Project Godlike. His dearth of empathy, his skillful facade of emotions, and his razor-sharp intellect rendered him the perfect candidate for a clandestine endeavor that demanded detachment and unyielding ruthlessness.

Cyrus had been scrutinized, his every nuance studied and manipulated, his sociopathic tendencies clandestinely nurtured. The perilous path I had chosen was one that demanded precision and vigilance, for I understood that sociopaths were unpredictable and prone to violence. Yet, these very qualities made Cyrus the ideal candidate for Project Godlike.

The covert project, shrouded in secrecy, was my endeavor to unlock the latent potential within Cyrus, powers inexorably linked to the abyss that dwelled within him. I had witnessed his capacity to manipulate and dominate others, to coerce them to his will. I believed that these attributes could be channeled into a force for good, a force capable of confronting the threat I had birthed.

Nonetheless, the weight of my actions, the manipulation of a young sociopath, lay heavy on my conscience. I had harnessed Cyrus's unique traits, driven by my agenda and priorities. The onus of this manipulation was mine to bear, a burden I could no longer overlook.

As I remained in my office, the intricate complexity of my choices loomed large, and the path to redemption was far from straightforward. The truth of Cyrus's sociopathy, his role in Project Godlike, would need to be unveiled in due course. It was imperative for him to make his own choices, guided by his moral compass... except he didn't have one.

Cyrus Finch

As I exited Dr. Creed's office, his words echoed in my mind, and I found myself lost in thought until Josh and Miguel abruptly yanked me from my reverie.

Inhale. Exhale. Inhale. Exhale.

Moments later, I turned a corner, and the deafening CRACK followed by shattering glass made me quicken my pace down the empty corridors of Seaview Academy. My mind couldn't help but drift to those horror movies where the characters meet their doom due to their own clumsiness. Was I destined to be one of those hapless souls, considering I had stayed in a nearly empty school building without much adult supervision?

Struggling to catch my breath, I desperately called out to the three bullies pursuing me, "Can I call a time out?" Inhale. Exhale. Inhale. Exhale. Inhale. Exhale. The lightheadedness washed over me like a relentless wave, and just before I tripped and tumbled in the hallway, it felt as if I were sliding into a foreboding abyss.

"He's asking for a time out," Josh quipped as he advanced toward me, a malevolent grin etched on his face, each step from his pristine white sneakers reverberating through the corridor.

For someone who seemingly only cared about sneakers, he seemed to take perverse pleasure in staining them with my blood. Tyrell, his faithful lackey, inched closer behind Josh's left side. "Should we grant his request?" Tyrell queried.

Josh shot Tyrell a withering look. "Is this a sport? Are we professional bullies? Where are the referees? What are the rules? Should you move to his side to even the odds? Think before you speak, man."

Tyrell hung his head, crushed by his failure to please his master, while Miguel, Josh's second lackey, relished the visible distress etched on Tyrell's face.

Exploiting their momentary distraction, I fumbled through my bag, frantically searching for my inhaler. My fingers finally closed around the cold metal, and as I retrieved it, a glimmer of hope surfaced; victory was within my grasp, and the name of the game was simply breathing.

CRACK.

The sound of breaking bones reverberated as my hand made a sound I had only associated with shattering ice. My inhaler soared out of my grasp, crashing into the wall, its fate mirroring my crushed hand.

I stared at my injured hand in disbelief, a surge of pain coursing through my arm, tears streaming down my face, and the act of breathing becoming an excruciating ordeal. It seemed that my life would be extinguished by the hands of these three tormentors.

"Pick him up," Josh commanded as he nonchalantly wiped the blood from his once-pristine white sneakers.

The two lackeys swiftly hoisted me up by my arms, my entire body trembling, my lungs working overtime, and the throbbing in my arms becoming unbearable. I fervently wished the pain in my arms would just cease.

Josh drew back his fist, poised to strike me in the stomach. "Wait, wait…" I stammered, prompting Josh to halt and arch an inquisitive eyebrow.

"What would Jesus do?" I offered with a sly smile, fully aware that this plea would fall on deaf ears.

Josh's fist collided with my stomach before I could utter another word, launching a relentless barrage of blows while he ranted about the perils of snitching and hurled every insult he could conjure. Amid the excruciating torment, one thought alone filled my mind: these two could double as pallbearers at my funeral.

There I stood, arms outstretched in a grotesque imitation of Mel Gibson in "The Passion of the Christ," pondering the potential economic prospects of my tormentors. I had once heard that the film was so graphic that someone had actually perished while watching it in the theater, presumably due to a heart attack.

HEART ATTACK.

A strange warmth surged through my veins, swiftly replaced by a chilling, icy sensation, and suddenly, I realized what I could do, what I had the power to do. I knew I could make them stop, permanently. I had to.

As I locked eyes with Tyrrell, I unleashed a venomous hatred in the form of a single word: "DIE."

Time ceased to be, with seconds stretching into eternities. Each breath seemed to unfurl like a never-ending 45-minute episode, painfully protracted. My vision blurred as my consciousness was transported to a different realm, while my body remained tethered to the cold, unforgiving marble floors of Seaview Academy.

In this altered state, my senses sharpened to an extraordinary degree. I could discern the acrid scent of burning asphalt from Exit 6 of the Staten Island Expressway. The cars on the highway moved in surreal slow motion, and I could even feel the wind gently rustling the grass against my...fur? The bizarre sensation of fur on my skin left me perplexed.

Before my bewildered senses, a crimson car streaked past the rest, coming to an abrupt halt, narrowly missing its intended exit. An 18-wheeler truck collided with the red sedan, crumpling it into a grotesque aluminum ball of destruction.

The cacophony of shattering glass, bones fracturing, and lungs being punctured assailed my heightened perception long before I could taste the metallic tang of blood in the air. A sense of horror engulfed me as I silently witnessed the tragedy unfolding before me, mingling the scent of my mother's perfume with the unmistakable stench of death.

My eyes gradually cleared as I was drawn back into my own body, feeling the scalding path of a solitary teardrop tracing down my cheek. Turning my gaze towards my next victim, I re-entered the realm of normal time. I found myself on the floor, hands and knees pressed against the cold, unforgiving marble.

A chilling sight awaited me as I looked over at Tyrrell. His lifeless body clenched his chest, his wide eyes frozen in the shock of his final moments. I shifted my attention back to Josh and Miguel, both now stricken with disbelief. However, it was clear that Tyrell's unexpected demise had ruptured the façade of toughness they had so meticulously cultivated.

The fear that gleamed in their eyes betrayed the vulnerability they had concealed beneath their ruthless exterior. The power I had unknowingly harnessed had shattered their world, leaving them exposed and terrified.

"DIE," I managed to choke out, my gaze locked on Miguel's terrified face as he slowly retreated from my relentless stare.

Once more, my eyes veiled in that exhilarating mist as the icy veins of power coursed through my body, dragging time into a creeping crawl. My consciousness slipped away, surrendering my vulnerable physical form to the dreary confines of the wretched school.

In the realm of my newfound authority, clarity struck me like a bolt of lightning. I beheld a man, as vivid as day, emerging from a bodega, consumed by optimism. He had just scratched off a winning lottery ticket, and the scent of his potent cologne pervaded my senses, even making my nose feel strangely...wet. But there was no time to ponder such oddities.

Overhead, construction workers operated a crane, maneuvering massive metal beams. Their cacophonous activity drowned out the man's exuberant victory shout, his jubilant dance, and ultimately, his cruel fate.

With a horrifying snap, the wire supporting one of the beams severed with lightning speed. I couldn't even identify the source of the deafening noise before the massive steel behemoth descended upon the man, crushing him against the building. The result was nothing more than a grotesque splatter.

Frozen in place, I bore witness to the unfolding tragedy, my horror boundless. A good Samaritan rushed to the scene, declaring, "I'm a med student!" as he clenched his winning ticket and pleaded for salvation.

A curious crowd began to assemble, their phones poised to capture the gruesome spectacle. The med student, with trembling hands, reached for his own phone and hastily dialed for help. He then checked the dying man's wrist for a pulse, only to pause in shock as his gaze fell upon the coveted ticket.

From the other end of the line, a calm yet experienced dispatcher inquired, "Hello, 911. Do you need police, fire, or medical assistance?" Her voice resonated through the phone with a detached professionalism.

Unbeknownst to the med student, he left the call active as he clutched the winning ticket. In the midst of despair, the man's body went limp as he breathed his last, surrendering all hope in humanity.

"Hello, is anybody there?" the dispatcher's voice inquired repeatedly. But the med student, his phone now vibrating in his pocket, had already begun his frantic sprint down the block, leaving behind a scene of tragedy that would forever haunt my thoughts.

Returning to the present, Miguel had been reduced to a horrific sight—a gory splatter on the floor, as though some cataclysmic force had atomized his body, leaving behind naught but a grotesque pool of thick, viscous blood. Any remnants of sadness had been purged, replaced by an all-consuming brew of contempt, hatred, and boiling anger.

In this moment, Josh remained, a mere shell of the bully he once was. He stood frozen in place, a visage of pure terror etched upon his face. His left leg quivered like a malfunctioning exercise device, and his eyes blinked rapidly, futilely warding off tears. The arrogant bravado and confidence he had once projected had disintegrated into nothingness. Josh was acutely aware that he could not hope to confront the formidable power I had come to embody—I was his god, and he, a helpless subject.

With trembling limbs, I slowly rose from the unforgiving floor, the throbbing agony in my hand underscoring the ordeal I had endured. Josh, unable to maintain his composure, collapsed to the ground, instantly giving in to despair, sobbing uncontrollably. The tears streaming down his face served as a poignant reminder of the countless sleepless nights I had endured at his hands, the ceaseless humiliation, and the unrelenting pain he had inflicted upon me.

"DIE," I uttered once more, yet there was no response, only bewilderment. I gazed down at my hands, then back up at Josh, who had been poised to charge at me.

"BREAK."

The familiar sensation of icy veins and decelerated time enveloped me, but this time, it was different. A blurry image flashed before my eyes—an enigmatic silhouette of a human figure with a crimson-glowing wrist. A distinct snap resounded in the chamber, accompanied by an unsettling sensation of something shifting within my own body, mending fragmented pieces.

My vision cleared, and I was unceremoniously thrust back into the harsh reality before me. Incredibly, my previously broken hand was now whole, leaving me stunned for several precious seconds.

The agonizing symphony of bones snapping, and Josh's shrill screams rudely jolted me back to reality. Strangely, the torment only served to amplify my sense of power.

I continued my measured approach toward Josh, halting just in front of his deteriorating form. His tear-soaked, snot-stained face begged for an end to his torment, his body twisting in agonizing contortions as his entire skeleton appeared to shatter in tandem.

"Enough," I finally sighed. Josh's tormented body stilled, leaving him a broken, pathetic heap, his own urine, sweat, and tears forming a vile pool around him. Mumbling to himself, he was but a shadow of his former self.

Stepping back, I turned to walk away, intending to exit the room before Josh could provoke a lethal response. Alas, my timing was less than perfect.

"Fucking pussy couldn't even finish the job," he jeered, causing me to halt mid-stride and slowly turn around.

"I'm sorry, I didn't catch that," I intoned, stopping in front of him once more. Josh met my gaze with trepidation. "I said..." he began.

Before he could finish, his teeth were ejected from his mouth, a direct result of my relentless assault. I continued to stomp upon his broken face with all my might, my body propelling into the air before crashing down. The sound of his skull shattering was deafening, leaving no doubt as to the gruesome outcome. An emotionless expression on his shattered visage told me everything I needed to know—I had emerged victorious.

DR Creed

Cyrus Finch shifted in his seat, his gaze piercing as he observed me, seemingly dissecting my very essence. Most would have felt violated under such scrutiny, but I was far from ordinary. No mere mortal could truly see through me.

"How did it feel, to win?" I inquired, my gaze steady on Cyrus, probing for any flicker of emotion.

"Powerful," he responded, his voice void of sentiment as his eyes locked onto mine.

"The deaths of those three boys made you feel powerful. Would you say that's a feeling you enjoyed?" I pressed, my tone unwavering.

Cyrus hesitated momentarily, for dramatic effect, though I knew he held the answer. He had gone from being the bullied to the oppressor in the blink of an eye, and the power must have been intoxicating. "I think I enjoyed the feeling of being back in control," he finally admitted.

I sighed, scribbling down some notes. "You killed three people, Cyrus. You were never in control."

Crimson tinged Cyrus's cheeks. "Tyrell died of a heart attack. It's not my fault bullying was too stressful for him."

I continued my writing, my pen gliding across the notepad. "What did you just write?" Cyrus inquired.

"Just some notes on our conversation," I replied, my gaze lifting to meet his. "Do you often deflect consequences with trivial jokes about serious matters?"

Cyrus met my question with silence, the unspoken tension hanging in the air. Just then, the phone rang, and I hastily picked up on the third ring, attentively listening.

"Okay. Thank you for sending it," I said before hanging up the phone and opening my laptop to check the first email.

"What was that about?" Cyrus asked, his curiosity apparent.

"Cyrus, I have a video of the incident," I explained. "I'd like you to narrate what happened so that I can fully grasp the context of what I'm about to watch."

Cyrus managed a mournful smile, an attempt at displaying remorse that failed to convince. He began to recount his story, detailing his ordeal of being bullied, with teardrops that seemed almost Oscar-worthy.

Cyrus Finch, a sociopath, more accurately diagnosed as having antisocial personality disorder, was entirely devoid of empathy and emotions. This made him a perfect candidate for our program. He possessed an exceptional intelligence, a hint of naivety, and a healthy dose of narcissism, allowing him to adeptly manipulate others into feeling sympathy.

I had read his extensive file, complete with the names of all fifty-seven doctors who had studied him and somehow declared him sane, even following the mysterious death of his pet dog. With his family's wealth, it was likely that some had been swayed by financial incentives, while others were merely inept.

My ability to operate outside the law afforded me a unique perspective on individuals like Cyrus, and now, we were about to delve into the heart of the matter.

I pressed play on the video, the absence of sound causing me no concern, given the extensive knowledge and experience I had acquired over thousands of years.

The video, complete with timestamps and color, displayed four windows showing various angles of the same L-shaped hallway. Middle school kids were engaged in a water fight, with Cyrus drenched after slipping on a puddle.

Miguel, Josh, and Tyrell soon converged upon him. As Cyrus reached into his bag, a small metal object caught my attention, drawing me to pause the video.

"Cyrus, did you have a switchblade?" I inquired, noting his reactions.

Cyrus shook his head. "No, that was my inhaler."

I pretended to skim his file for effect. "It doesn't mention asthma in your records."

Cyrus grinned smugly. "I guess your file doesn't know everything."

I knew he was lying, and I was determined to uncover the truth. "Cyrus, please continue your story, especially about the icy feeling in your veins."

I resumed the video, Cyrus's gaze locking onto Tyrell. His body stiffened, and moments later, Tyrell suffered a heart attack. Josh and Miguel retreated in fear as Tyrell collapsed.

Cyrus experienced another icy episode, and soon after, Miguel met a gruesome fate, exploding in a shower of gore.

Josh, further down the hallway, slipped on the wet floor and collided with the wall. As Cyrus approached, still nursing his injured wrist, Josh's body contorted and broke.

Two minutes of torment followed before Josh's ordeal ceased. Cyrus walked away down the hallway, leaving Josh in a pitiful state.

However, Cyrus turned back, retrieved the switchblade from the floor, and returned to Josh. He stood above his victim, his foot delivering a devastating blow to Josh's face, propelling his sneaker away. Cyrus then rained down a series of merciless stabs into Josh's chest, as though he were playing the most brutal video game.

The video ended, and I removed my glasses, rubbing my eyes with weariness. "That was quite the spectacle," I commented. "The video portrays a different narrative from your account, Cyrus. While their actions may have been excessive, I'm not convinced they deserved death. I'm also uncertain about the exact cause of their demise. Tyrell may have suffered a heart attack, but Josh was undeniably murdered by you."

Cyrus met my gaze, his expression a blend of defiance and resignation.

"I killed all three of them," he admitted, devoid of remorse or guilt. His disappointment at getting caught overshadowed any feelings of guilt or remorse.

I shook my head, addressing his unspoken impulse problem. Cyrus Finch might have been a sociopath, but he was a puzzle I was eager to unravel.

I leaned forward in my chair, my expression unyielding as I locked eyes with Cyrus Finch. "Cyrus, you may have killed them, but you also inadvertently brought us together. My purpose here is not only to understand but to help you."

A hint of curiosity flickered in his otherwise emotionless gaze. "Help me? What can you do?"

"It's a long road," I replied, tapping the thick file I had brought with me. "A path that may offer you a semblance of control and understanding over your impulses. But it's a path that will require your cooperation and commitment."

Cyrus, ever the manipulator, appeared to consider the offer. He might be devoid of genuine emotions, but the allure of control and power over his own destiny was tempting, even for someone like him.

I continued, "Cyrus, the video we watched tells a different story. It raises questions about the nature of your abilities and their origin. There's much we can explore and understand together, but it begins with your willingness to be open and truthful."

Cyrus's eyes held mine for a moment, and then he nodded, a slight smile playing on his lips. "I'm willing to cooperate."

"Good," I said, feeling a glimmer of hope. This might be the breakthrough we had been searching for. "We'll begin by unraveling your past, your abilities, and the mysteries surrounding your actions. It won't be easy, but it's a path to reclaim some semblance of control."

"So, when do we start?" Cyrus asked.

CYRUS FINCH

As I looked around the mysterious and imposing Godlike facility, I couldn't help but feel like a stranger in a strange land. The notion of Dr. Creed's secretive military school for individuals like me seemed like something straight out of a science fiction novel. The path that had led me here was filled with extraordinary events, all of which had culminated in the puzzling revelation of my own abilities.

It all began with my beloved dog, Chase. He had been my constant companion throughout my formative years, a loyal and affectionate friend who had seen me through the best and worst times of my life. So when he fell victim to cancer, it was as if a piece of my heart had been cruelly torn away. The overwhelming helplessness I felt spurred me to embark on a quest for a solution, one that led me down a path I never could have foreseen.

Chase's illness was a formidable adversary, one that had struck down even the most skilled veterinarians. It was a relentless opponent, and I couldn't bear the thought of losing him. Desperation drove me to seek alternatives beyond conventional medicine, and it was in the depths of my despair that I uncovered the ancient legends of the inugami.

Inugami, dog spirits of immense power, were rumored to have the ability to heal and protect their masters. As I delved into the obscure rituals and texts surrounding these creatures, I found myself consumed by the possibility of saving Chase. The process was shrouded in mystery and mysticism, a far cry from the rational world I had known.

The day I performed the ritual that would alter the course of my life forever was etched into my memory. I recited the incantations and followed the ancient instructions with a mixture of hope and doubt. There was an eerie feeling in the air, a sense of anticipation that I couldn't explain. And then, as the last words left my lips, an inexplicable force enveloped me.

Chase's recovery was nothing short of miraculous. The cancer that had plagued him seemed to vanish overnight, and his health was restored. Yet, the enigmatic process had left an indelible mark on him. He had become something more than a regular dog, a guardian bound to me in a way I couldn't fully comprehend.

It wasn't until later that I discovered the full extent of the changes that had occurred. Chase had become an inugami, a creature that could be commanded to perform extraordinary feats. This revelation sent shockwaves through my family, who were both amazed and horrified by the revelation. They chose to keep my discovery a secret, leveraging their wealth and influence to protect me from the consequences of my actions.

But the powers I had unlocked were not without their dark side. The day I had first exercised my newfound abilities to save Chase's life was the same day I had unknowingly condemned my family to a tragic fate. The thought that my actions had led to their deaths weighed heavily on my conscience, and it was a burden I could never shake.

Now, I found myself at the Godlike facility, a place that seemed like the epicenter of an unfolding cosmic drama. I had been transferred here at the request of Dr. Creed, a man who exuded an aura of mystery and authority. His enigmatic project, known as "Godlike," was a daunting prospect, and I couldn't help but wonder how I fit into this extraordinary puzzle.

On my first day, I was accompanied by Alice, a scout who had been sent to my previous school to identify individuals with unique abilities. She was a lively and engaging presence, a stark contrast to the ominous nature of the facility. As we explored the labyrinthine halls of Godlike, Alice explained the grand vision of Dr. Creed.

She portrayed him as a benevolent philanthropist dedicated to a singular mission – to find someone or something strong enough to prevent the end of the world. The weight of that responsibility seemed to press down on my shoulders, and the daunting prospect of such a monumental task left me both intrigued and apprehensive.

Alice's enthusiasm was palpable, and I couldn't help but wonder about her role in this grand endeavor. "So, Cyrus, you've been chosen for this project because Dr. Creed believes there's more to your abilities than you might think. You have a rare gift, and it might hold the key to saving the world."

I couldn't conceal my apprehension. "But you don't understand, Alice. I don't have powers anymore. The last time I used them, my family... they all died the same day. I haven't been able to use them since."

Alice regarded me with a mixture of empathy and curiosity. She seemed unfazed by my revelation, as if she had encountered countless individuals with their own extraordinary stories. "Cyrus, sometimes these abilities are tied to our emotions and experiences. It's possible that it's not a lack of power but a psychological barrier holding you back. You may need to confront your past to regain control."

Her words hung in the air, a reminder of the traumatic events that had reshaped my life. I couldn't help but consider the possibility that I had allowed my fear and guilt to imprison my own abilities.

Alice went on to explain the nature of these powers – the ability to kill with mere words, to manipulate reality through spoken commands. She emphasized that such abilities were not to be wielded lightly, as they came with a cost. The universe, she explained, demanded an equivalent exchange for each use of these powers.

As I listened to her, I couldn't help but contemplate the gravity of what lay ahead. The prospect of wielding powers of such magnitude was both alluring and terrifying. The mysterious universe and its intricate balance seemed like a riddle that I was only beginning to unravel.

I took a deep breath, a sense of determination building within me. The challenges and mysteries that awaited me at the Godlike facility were vast and daunting, but I couldn't ignore the call to embrace my extraordinary abilities and confront the shadows of my past. Dr. Creed's project held the potential to save the world, and I was determined to discover whether I could rise to the occasion and unlock the dormant power within me.

Alice's tour of the Godlike facility was nothing short of surreal. She led me through hallways filled with extraordinary individuals, each with their own unique abilities. It was a mesmerizing and bewildering experience, and my mind reeled as I tried to process the staggering potential of the project in which I had become entangled.

The tour took an unexpected turn as Alice brought me to a massive underground fighting ring. A throng of onlookers had gathered, their excitement palpable. In the center of the arena, two figures prepared for an epic showdown. On one side stood a young man whose body crackled with flames, his eyes radiating a fierce intensity. On the opposite end, a woman in an elegant yet mysterious attire had an aura of alchemical power surrounding her. The stage was set for a battle that promised to be nothing short of spectacular.

Alice's voice cut through the charged atmosphere. "Cyrus, this is one of the core aspects of the Godlike project. It's about enhancing the warrior gene, a gene that, when mutated, unlocks latent abilities in a person, granting them godlike powers over a specific domain. The battles that take place here help these individuals harness and refine their abilities."

I couldn't take my eyes off the unfolding spectacle. The man with fire abilities conjured blazing infernos, his control over flames awe-inspiring. His opponent, the alchemist, seemed to manipulate matter itself, transmuting elements into weapons and defenses with grace and precision.

The battle that ensued was a breathtaking dance of power, finesse, and strategy. The fire-wielder launched searing projectiles while the alchemist countered with shimmering barriers of elemental transmutations. The audience was spellbound by the sheer beauty and spectacle of the fight, as sparks and flames danced with swirling eddies of liquid metal.

As the battle raged on, the contenders pushed their abilities to the limit. The fire-wielder unleashed an incandescent blaze, searing the arena with radiant heat. In response, the alchemist channeled her power, transforming the very air into a torrent of shimmering water to extinguish the flames. The arena was a symphony of chaos and harmony, a collision of elemental forces.

But the climax of the battle lay in the final moments. With a burst of power that resonated through the entire arena, the alchemist transmuted the ground beneath her into a bladed storm of crystalline shards. She sent them hurtling toward the fire-wielder with precision and speed. In a daring last move, he created a fiery vortex, trying to disintegrate the shards.

The result was a breathtaking collision of fire and ice, a dazzling clash of elements. The two forces met in an explosive display, and for a fleeting instant, the arena was illuminated with a blinding brilliance.

The aftermath of the battle was nothing short of astonishing. The alchemist stood victorious, having outmaneuvered her fiery adversary with sheer ingenuity and skill. The audience erupted into thunderous applause and cheers, celebrating the display of godlike abilities that had unfolded before them.

As the combatants embraced in a show of mutual respect, the crowd began to disperse, their awe-filled conversations filling the air. It was then that I realized the scale and significance of the project I had been drawn into. The warrior gene, its mutations, and the godlike powers it could unlock were all part of a grand design to save the world from impending catastrophe.

The epic conclusion of the battle had revealed to me the extraordinary potential of those within the Godlike facility. They were not just individuals with abilities but heroes, honing their powers to become something greater. I had taken my first steps into a world where the boundaries of human potential were being rewritten, and I couldn't help but wonder how I might fit into this extraordinary tapestry of abilities and destinies.

Dr Creed

My office was shrouded in an aura of solemnity as I engaged in a private conversation with Alice. The gentle hum of the overhead lights seemed to emphasize the gravity of our discussion, and the room exuded an almost surreal atmosphere.

Leaning forward in my leather chair, I locked my gaze on Alice with the weight of centuries of knowledge and secrets behind my eyes. "Alice, I brought Cyrus into the program for a very specific reason. I saw in him a unique potential, someone who could navigate the intricate realms of godlike powers with precision and control."

Alice, youthful and vibrant, nodded in understanding. "I trust your judgment, Dr. Creed. But I've been curious about one thing—why me? Why did you choose me to scout Cyrus?"

I let out a sigh and leaned back, my thoughts drifting for a moment. "Cyrus has a history, a history that I believe may hold the key to our salvation. To explain, I must reveal a part of my past that very few have ever heard."

I continued, my voice steady, "Many years ago, long before you joined this program, I was close friends with a guardian named Peter Wayne. He was among the best, a guardian of the highest caliber, and we faced challenges that most would never comprehend. I was there with him every step of the way."

Alice leaned forward, sensing the profound personal story I was about to share.

"We encountered a formidable adversary," I continued, "and in a situation where we had to make an unimaginable decision, I was compelled to terminate Peter."

Alice's surprise was evident. "You had to kill your own friend?"

I nodded solemnly. "Yes, it was a painful and traumatic experience. I watched Peter die, and I watched his soul start to leave his body. But I couldn't accept it. I couldn't let go of my friend. His death weighed heavily on my soul."

I allowed my gaze to drift, lost in the haunting memories of the past. "So, I did something that defied all logic and reason. I placed a nogitsune into Peter's lifeless body, a creature capable of manipulating energy. It was a desperate attempt to save my friend."

Alice frowned, puzzled. "A nogitsune? You put that into your friend's body?"

I nodded again, my voice heavy with regret. "But it wasn't just any nogitsune, Alice. It was different. My actions created a being I call Moros Noctis. He's a nogitsune that feeds off the residual energy of Uriel, the archangel of God's wrath. In other words, he's powered by divine fury."

The revelation hit Alice like a bolt of lightning. "So, you created one of the most powerful beings in existence?"

My voice was filled with remorse. "Yes, and that power terrifies me. But Moros Noctis saved me from the corrupting influence of my own actions. He kept me from becoming a monster, and I've tried to ensure he walks a path of restraint and control."

Understanding the gravity of the situation, Alice said, "And you believe Cyrus is the key to this somehow?"

I leaned forward, my expression intense. "I do. I believe that Cyrus, with his unique ability to control and manipulate others through his words, might be the only one capable of helping Moros Noctis find the balance we desperately need. We are at the brink of a catastrophic event, and if we don't succeed in reining in Moros Noctis, I don't know what the consequences will be. We need someone who can speak to the very heart of power."

Alice's gaze was filled with determination. "I'll do everything in my power to assist Cyrus and ensure we avert this catastrophe."

I nodded, a sense of urgency in my eyes. "Thank you, Alice. Our very existence is at stake, and it will take all of us working together to find the answers we need."

Our pact was sealed, a bond of dedication to avert impending catastrophe, and the weight of our roles in the Godlike program became more apparent than ever. With Moros Noctis's presence lurking in the background, we knew that the battle to safeguard the world had become even more treacherous and uncertain.

The weight of our conversation settled heavily in the room as the future of our world hung in the balance. Alice and I had pledged to work together to avert the looming catastrophe, but there were still dark secrets I hadn't revealed. My true motives for bringing Cyrus into the program were far more complex than I had let on.

As our discussion concluded, I knew that our journey was far from over. The fate of our world hung in the balance, and we had just embarked on a perilous path to salvation.

Samuel Creed, a name that had held many secrets and one that I had taken on, had recruited and manipulated Cyrus Finch for a specific purpose - one that wasn't solely about communicating with Moros Noctis, as I had led Alice to believe. There was a deeper, more sinister motive behind my actions. Cyrus was the key to achieving a mission that had weighed on my conscience for years.

My plans had been shrouded in shadows, and Cyrus was now an unwitting pawn in a game he couldn't possibly comprehend. The inugami that he possessed was not just a means of communication with Moros Noctis; it was a weapon, a weapon that had the potential to destroy the very essence of my creation.

With a heavy heart, I glanced at Alice, who had unwaveringly committed to assisting Cyrus. She was unaware of the true nature of the task that lay ahead.

I knew that I had to reveal the depths of my intentions to her. I owed her that much, for she had been a loyal and dedicated ally throughout our endeavors. But with the fate of the world hanging in the balance, there was no room for half-truths and hidden agendas.

"Alice," I began, my voice tinged with a sense of gravity, "there is something I must confess. My purpose in recruiting Cyrus goes beyond communication with Moros Noctis."

Alice looked at me, her brow furrowing in confusion. "What do you mean, Dr. Creed?"

Taking a deep breath, I revealed the dark truth. "I intend to use Cyrus's inugami, not to converse with Moros Noctis, but to eliminate him. To kill him."

The room seemed to grow colder, and the gravity of my words settled in. I continued, "Moros Noctis is not just a creature of immense power; he's a threat to the very fabric of our existence. He was created out of desperation, much like the inugami, and his presence poses a danger that I can no longer ignore."

Alice's eyes widened, and she processed the weight of my revelation. "But, Dr. Creed, can we be sure that Cyrus's inugami is capable of such a task?"

I nodded, my determination unwavering. "The inugami is a natural enemy of kitsunes, including nogitsunes like Moros Noctis. It possesses the ability to track and destroy them. I've taken measures to ensure Cyrus's inugami is powerful enough to confront this formidable threat."

The room was filled with an uneasy silence as Alice grappled with the magnitude of our mission. "So, our goal is not just to communicate with Moros Noctis, but to eradicate him completely?"

I nodded once more, my gaze steady. "Yes, Alice. To safeguard our world, we must rid it of Moros Noctis. The consequences of his existence are far too dire."

With newfound determination, Alice squared her shoulders. "Then, we must prepare Cyrus for the task ahead. We'll need his unique abilities to ensure the inugami's success in this mission."

Our pact had evolved, the stakes had risen, and our roles had taken on a new significance. We were no longer seeking to communicate with a powerful being but to face it head-on and eliminate the threat it posed.

As Alice and I left the confines of my office, the weight of the revelation lingered in the air. Our mission had taken a darker turn, and we were heading to observe Cyrus's training session with Maximus, one of the proteges of Project Godlike.

The training grounds were a sprawling facility filled with combat arenas, and amidst the clashing sounds of battle, we found Cyrus engaged in close quarters combat with Maximus. The difference in their abilities was glaring; Maximus moved with a grace and precision that Cyrus was yet to attain.

Every time Cyrus was knocked to the ground, Maximus offered advice and constructive criticism, a mentor attempting to shape his protege into a formidable force. I watched with a keen eye, recognizing the necessity for Cyrus to become stronger if he were to face the looming threat of Moros Noctis.

As their sparring continued, Cyrus struggled to gain an upper hand. Maximus was an experienced and talented fighter, and it was evident that his tutelage was pushing Cyrus to his limits. With each clash, he was learning, but the road to mastering his inugami was a challenging one.

During the pauses between rounds, Alice and I discussed Cyrus's progress and the urgency of our mission. "How long do you think it will take for Cyrus to be ready, Dr. Creed?" Alice asked, her gaze never leaving the combatants.

I considered her question carefully. "It's difficult to determine an exact timeframe, but we must expedite his training. We're running out of time, and the fate of our world depends on it. The experiment cannot be delayed."

The words weighed heavily on us as we watched Cyrus's determination, his will to become stronger. It was a necessary transformation, but the urgency of our situation left little room for error.

As the training session pressed on, frustration seemed to mount within Cyrus. He locked eyes with Maximus and, in a moment of raw anger, screamed, "Die."

A hushed silence fell upon the arena as the room tensed with anticipation. Yet, nothing happened. Cyrus's abilities, the very powers that had unnerved us, failed to manifest, leaving him bewildered.

Enraged by what Cyrus had attempted, Maximus turned to him, his voice trembling with anger, and demanded, "Did you just try to kill me?" With brutal determination, Maximus unleashed his telekinesis, throwing Cyrus around the room in a violent display of power.

I stood there, my thoughts racing. "Cyrus... what have you done?"

Alice looked at me, her concern mirrored in her eyes. "Dr. Creed, could he have killed Maximus with his inugami?"

I shook my head, a grim realization dawning on me. "No, Alice. It seems that Cyrus's abilities have not fully manifested, and I have a theory as to why."

Maximus continued his brutal assault on Cyrus, his rage unrelenting, as we contemplated the root of Cyrus's incomplete powers. My theory took shape, a hypothesis that suggested the inugami's efficacy was tied to a grim and haunting aspect of its nature.

"The inugami," I began, my voice strained, "has a trade-off for the lives it takes. It demands the exchange of loved ones, a price that Cyrus may not have paid."

As the two proteges clashed in the training ring, a dark cloud of uncertainty loomed over us. The road to harnessing Cyrus's powers was becoming more treacherous, and the realization that the inugami demanded sacrifices for its abilities added an eerie layer to our already perilous journey.

CYRUS FINCH

I couldn't remember a time when I'd been pushed so far, physically and mentally, while being utterly powerless. Maximus's fury knew no bounds as he continued to pummel me relentlessly. Each blow landed with a force that felt like a freight train, throwing me around the training room like a rag doll.

As I tried to come up with a strategy to counter Maximus's brutal assault, the words "Die" still echoed in my mind. The power I had tried to wield against him was gone, and the consequence of that reckless act was a merciless beatdown that left me gasping for breath.

My attempts to defend myself had become futile. Maximus, driven by rage, continued to unleash a relentless assault, and I was left with no option but to keep moving, ducking, and evading to avoid being obliterated by his powerful strikes.

Maximus's overpowering fury left me vulnerable and overwhelmed. Blow after blow landed with crushing force, and I struggled to find an opening, any opportunity to turn the tide of the fight. Maximus's overpowering fury left me vulnerable and overwhelmed. Every blow felt like a sledgehammer slamming into me, and I had to rely on every ounce of my instinct and training to keep from crumbling.

His telekinesis was like an invisible vice, each construct he conjured a testament to his overwhelming power. I barely had time to react as they came at me, one after another, striking with the precision and force of a battering ram. They hit me from every direction, sending me spinning through the air like a leaf in a storm.

The pain was excruciating, my body felt like it was being torn apart. I fought to stay conscious, to find a way out of this relentless assault, but I could hardly think through the torrent of pain.

My mind raced, searching for a strategy, an opening. But Maximus allowed no respite, his fury a relentless tempest that showed no sign of abating. I was no match for his sheer strength, and with each strike, I felt my confidence wane.

Blow after blow, Maximus was determined to make me pay for the attempt on his life. As my body absorbed each crushing impact, I couldn't help but wonder if there was an end to this relentless onslaught.

Maximus encased himself in a formidable armor forged from telekinetic constructs. This armor, coupled with his kinetic sword, made him an unstoppable force. He advanced on me with unyielding ferocity, and I realized that there was nowhere to run, no escape from this brutal punishment.

Each swing of the kinetic sword came like a blade cutting through my defenses. Blow after blow landed, the ground shuddering beneath the force of the impact. I was sent hurtling into the ground, the earth itself seeming to shake as I crashed down.

My vision swayed, stars dancing before my eyes. Pain coursed through every fiber of my being, and I gasped for breath, trying to regain my senses. The arena was spinning around me, and the sounds of battle seemed distant, as if muffled by the weight of my actions and the price I was paying for them.

Maximus, looming over me, was a relentless force, and I could see the determination in his eyes. It was clear he wanted me to pay for my actions, and he was willing to exact that payment through each punishing blow.

Finally, as I lay on the ground, disoriented and battered, with no defense left. Maximus, fueled by his fury, prepared to deliver a final, devastating blow. The arena was filled with tension, and I could see the deadly arc of his attack bearing down upon me. My heart raced as I braced for the inevitable impact.

In that crucial moment, the tension in the arena was unbearable. As Maximus swung down the massive telekinetic sword to deliver a potentially lethal blow, I felt the crushing weight of my powerlessness and vulnerability.

The seconds stretched into eternity, and it was then, in the most desperate moment of the fight, that something inexplicable occurred. A ripple, like a fracture in time and space itself, suddenly materialized in the room, and through it emerged Elijah Wayne, the highest-ranking Godlike agent in the world.

Elijah's presence was unlike anything I had ever experienced. As he stepped into the arena, the very surroundings seemed to respond to his extraordinary power. The air hummed with an energy that came to life, and even the most lifeless objects around us, the specks of dust, the stones, and even the faded mats on the floor, appeared to burst with new vitality. It was as if he brought life to everything he touched.

Maximus, frozen mid-strike, was the first to witness Elijah's arrival. His towering fury, which had moments ago been directed at me, seemed to vanish as he dropped to one knee in a submissive gesture.

The hushed astonishment in the room was palpable. Elijah Wayne's presence commanded a reverence that was almost spiritual in nature. He held himself with an aura of authority that left no room for doubt or defiance.

Maximus dared not move a muscle, and the rest of us could only watch in silent awe as Elijah effortlessly deflected the impending blow from Maximus's telekinetic sword. The clash of forces between Maximus and Elijah created a shockwave that reverberated through the arena, and the resounding impact could be felt by everyone present.

Elijah's gaze, as he regarded Maximus, was unwavering. It was as if he could see into the very soul of the man who had just moments ago been my assailant. The energy in the room seemed to align with his presence, and for that brief moment, the world felt different, as though we were standing on the precipice of a newfound understanding of power.

Silence hung heavily in the air as Elijah finally broke his gaze and spoke. His voice, resonant and authoritative, cut through the stillness. "The fight is over."

His words, though simple, were imbued with an undeniable finality, and everyone within earshot felt their impact. Elijah's gaze swept across the room, and it was then that the tension in the atmosphere began to dissipate, like a storm finally yielding to the calm.

Dr. Creed nodded in acknowledgment and gratitude towards Elijah, a silent "thank you" that held a world of meaning. It was clear that the battle in the arena had been halted not only to protect me but also to ensure that Maximus didn't cross a line he couldn't return from.

With a profound sense of relief and reverence for Elijah Wayne, I knew that I had much to learn from this extraordinary figure. I yearned to understand the depths of what it meant to be a Godlike, to attain the level of power and presence that he effortlessly embodied. This moment would remain etched in my memory as the day I was spared by the intervention of the most powerful agent in the world, a day that would forever change the course of my training and my understanding of what it meant to possess godlike abilities.

Slowly, I managed to rise from the ground, my body protesting every movement. As I stood unsteadily, my eyes fixed on Elijah. He gazed at me with an intensity that was both unsettling and captivating.

"You need to get stronger," Elijah declared, his voice carrying a weight that demanded attention. "If you ever attempt to harm any of my agents again, I will not hesitate to rip you apart, slowly and methodically. And once that's done, Alice will place you in a hellish illusion for eternity. Do we understand each other?"

The threat hung in the air, its severity sending shivers down my spine. I could only nod, realizing the gravity of my actions and the consequences if I strayed from the path of control and discipline.

Elijah's demeanor shifted immediately, and he gestured for me to follow him. "Come, let's go eat."

We moved from the arena to a nearby dining area, and I was keenly aware of the enigmatic figure walking by my side. There was an air of mystery that clung to Elijah, but he gave no indication of what powers he possessed.

As we sat down, he began to explain the transformation process. "Today is your day. It's when every Godlike agent undergoes their transformation to receive their powers. You'll be pushed to your limits, both physically and mentally. It's a process of awakening your true potential."

I couldn't help but be intrigued, and I seized the opportunity to ask about Elijah's own powers. "What abilities do you have?"

Elijah chuckled lightly, as if my question was amusing. "I'm pretty normal compared to the people around here. You'll soon see what I mean. Each Godlike agent is ranked based on their powers, and training can be quite rigorous."

He went on to explain the hierarchy among Godlike agents, where those with more potent powers held higher ranks. It was a complex system that dictated the dynamics within the organization.

We finished our meal, and Elijah stood, indicating that it was time to proceed with the transformation process. As we made our way to the chambers, I couldn't help but feel a mix of anticipation and trepidation. Waiting for us at the entrance was Dr. Creed, a man who seemed to hold the knowledge and secrets of an entire world within his enigmatic gaze.

Dr. Creed opened the door to the chambers, and it felt like crossing a threshold into the unknown. The room was filled with an otherworldly aura, shimmering with a faint, ethereal light. It was here, in this sacred space, that the transformation process would take place.

As I entered, a sense of reverence washed over me. The walls were adorned with intricate symbols and patterns, and a palpable energy thrummed in the air. The anticipation and gravity of the moment weighed on me as I stepped further into the heart of the chamber.

Elijah and Dr. Creed followed, their presence grounding me in this extraordinary experience. Dr. Creed spoke in a tone that resonated with wisdom and authority. "Cyrus, you are about to embark on a journey of self-discovery and power. This transformation will unlock the potential that lies dormant within you, granting you abilities beyond imagination. But remember, power without control can be dangerous."

I nodded, absorbing his words and the weight of my responsibilities as a future Godlike agent. This process was not only about gaining extraordinary abilities but also about harnessing them responsibly.

Elijah, with his piercing gaze, added, "This is your moment, Cyrus. Embrace it with focus and determination. You'll be tested in ways you've never imagined, but you have the potential to become one of us, a guardian of humanity."

Their words served as a solemn reminder of the path I had chosen. I was ready to face the challenges that lay ahead. Dr. Creed raised his hand, and the symbols on the walls began to glow with a soft, radiant light.

The transformation process had begun, and my journey as a Godlike agent was set in motion. I couldn't predict the trials and revelations that awaited me, but I was prepared to embrace them with open arms, driven by the belief that I could make a difference in a world teetering on the brink of uncertainty.

DR CREED

Elijah's hands pressed gently against Cyrus's battered and bruise body, and as the two men made contact, a soft, radiant glow enveloped the younger man. Instantly, the wounds and bruises that had marked Cyrus's form began to disappear. The pain that had gripped him just moments earlier ebbed away, as if it had never existed. I watched in silent awe as Elijah's healing touch worked its magic, the wounds vanishing and the bruises fading, leaving Cyrus's skin unblemished once more.

With the healing process complete, I guided Cyrus into a chamber designed specifically for the transformative procedure. The glass door sealed shut, securing him inside. I stepped out, followed by Elijah, and our departure marked the arrival of a team of scientists who were well-versed in the intricate procedures that lay ahead. The chamber room hummed with a sense of anticipation as they entered, donned in their white lab coats and armed with a deep knowledge of the complex processes that would soon unfold.

Cyrus's eyes flickered with a mixture of anxiety and uncertainty as he observed the scientists preparing for the transformative procedure. Intricate tubes and wires snaked through the chamber, ready to deliver precise measurements of fluids and gases into his veins. It was a surreal sight, and Cyrus, a novice in this world of immense power, couldn't help but feel a growing sense of trepidation.

As the scientists moved with a blend of precision and confidence, the tension in the chamber mounted. Their meticulous checks, the pressing of buttons, and the continuous monitoring of the intricate computer screens painted a picture of a crucial operation, fraught with both risk and potential. The scientific equipment, complex and advanced, was primed to deliver its payload and unlock the untapped potential within Cyrus.

Cyrus's anxiety and the sense of foreboding seemed to intensify as the experiment commenced. The fluids and gas began their journey through his veins, their precise orchestration triggering a series of complex reactions in his body. Cyrus's form trembled and convulsed with the intensity of the process, his expressions contorted with agony and disbelief. I stood behind the reinforced glass, my eyes focused intently on the procedure, making notations on a digital pad as I observed Cyrus's transformation.

The scientists in the chamber room worked diligently, their eyes glued to the multiple screens, adjusting the parameters as necessary. The high stakes of the experiment were unmistakable, and it was clear that there were no guarantees that it could be halted without potential consequences. The room's atmosphere was fraught with uncertainty as they toiled to ensure that the transformation proceeded without a hitch.

Cyrus's cries of agony grew louder, echoing through the chamber. He was now at the mercy of a transformative process that delved deep into the core of his being. The convulsions, the agony, and the impending metamorphosis were a formidable mix, and they bore down upon him with unremitting intensity.

Inside the chamber room, the frantic beeping of the computers provided a discordant symphony to the unfolding drama. The scientists exchanged concerned glances, unsure of whether to continue the experiment or to halt it and prevent further harm to Cyrus. Their faces were etched with doubt, and they looked to me for guidance, their unspoken questions hanging heavily in the air.

In response to their queries, I held my ground and instructed them to continue. The transformation was a pivotal step in Cyrus's journey to becoming a Godlike agent, and there was no turning back. The cost was steep, but the potential rewards were immeasurable.

As Cyrus's pain reached its peak, a sudden shift in the chamber's atmosphere signaled the activation of his inugami. The invisible force surged to life; a tempest of raw energy unleashed in response to his torment. It tore through the chamber like a vengeful specter, wreaking havoc as if the very air had come to life.

The scientists, caught off guard by the sudden eruption of power, had no chance to react. They were ensnared by the maelstrom, their bodies torn apart with merciless brutality, their expressions frozen in shock and pain. In the wake of this carnage, the chamber fell silent, a stark contrast to the chaos that had unfolded just moments ago.

Behind the reinforced glass, I stared at the horrific scene with a mix of awe and trepidation. The computers, still emitting their shrill beeping, indicated that the experiment had reached its 100 percent completion. The transformative process had come at a great cost, and Cyrus's journey into the world of the Godlike had taken a harrowing turn.

Without a moment's hesitation, I took out my phone, my voice calm but resolute as I spoke into it, "We need a clean-up in the chamber rooms." The aftermath was a stark reminder of the boundless power and potential danger that the Godlike agents held within them, and the responsibilities that lay ahead for Cyrus were monumental.   As the echo of my calm instruction lingered in the chamber room, the door swung open, and a clean-up crew rushed in. Their arrival was swift and efficient, a well-practiced routine that dealt with the aftermath of this transformative procedure. Wearing protective suits, they began the somber task of removing the lifeless bodies of the scientists who had met their untimely end in this chamber of power and potential.

Their movements were methodical, and the chamber room quickly transformed from a scene of chaos to one of solemn order. It was a chilling reminder of the cost that could accompany the unlocking of extraordinary abilities.

Amidst this morbid operation, another group of agents arrived. These were not part of the clean-up crew but a more solemn contingent, armed and focused. Their mission was clear - to transport Cyrus to a solitary cell, a move designed to ensure the safety of all involved. Cyrus, still unconscious from the tumultuous transformation process, lay prone on a medical dolly, unresponsive to the world around him.

I watched with a furrowed brow, deep in thought, as the agents wheeled him out of the chamber. The solitude of the cell would provide an opportunity to recover and, more importantly, to contain the power that now coursed through him. The transition was swift and efficient, a testament to the orderliness of the Godlike organization.

Once Cyrus had been secured in his temporary sanctuary, the door closed with a resounding thud. He was now isolated from the outside world, a necessary step to both protect him and those around him. The weight of his journey had taken on new gravity, and his future as a Godlike agent had never seemed so uncertain.

Outside the chamber room, a hushed discussion took place among the agents. Concerns and questions hung in the air, but there were few answers. The events that had transpired were unprecedented, leaving us grappling with the mysteries of Cyrus's inugami activation.

I couldn't help but ponder what had just unfolded. The inugami was known to barter for the lives of a Godlike agent's loved ones in exchange for its devastating power, yet Cyrus had no such connections, no loved ones for the entity to claim. The means by which it had been invoked remained a baffling enigma, defying the rules and expectations that had governed our understanding of these mystical bonds between human and inugami.

The ramifications of this incident were far-reaching, and the depths of the supernatural world had once again proven their impenetrable complexity. In the wake of this ordeal, a daunting realization settled in my mind: the path ahead for Cyrus was marked by challenges more profound than I had ever anticipated, and the darkness of uncertainty shrouded our understanding of his unique abilities.

Cyrus Finch

Throughout those weeks, I remained in solitary confinement, my mind haunted by the enigmatic circumstances of my transformation. I was visited by Alice, the one familiar face that provided a fleeting connection to the world outside. She was my lifeline in the desolation of my cell, offering conversations that both intrigued and puzzled me.

Alice shared stories from Japanese folklore, mesmerizing me with tales of legendary figures, folklore heroes, and the larger-than-life exploits of superheroes. Her vivid descriptions and her ability to cast illusions brought her narratives to life within the sterile walls of my cell.

However, it was not just the fantastical stories she told that captivated me. In our interactions, I began to admire her unwavering dedication to the Godlike program, her determination to protect the world from incomprehensible threats. Her purpose and drive were evident in every word she spoke.

Despite the enchanting tales and Alice's unwavering commitment, my thoughts remained tethered to a mystery I couldn't solve. I didn't understand the inner workings of my own abilities or what triggered the enigmatic inugami within me. It was a source of profound confusion and unease.

As we explored these captivating narratives, we delved into both the grand and the ordinary moments of life, sharing experiences, hopes, and dreams. Alice's illusions transformed the mundane into something extraordinary, allowing me to experience the authenticity of human connection, even within the confines of my isolation.

The stories became my lifeline, a temporary escape from the solace that threatened to engulf me. I held on to the hope that, in our shared moments, I might someday unlock the secrets of my newfound powers, understanding them as Alice understood her own strength and unwavering commitment to the Godlike cause.

Alice and I continued our conversations, and over time, I began to see the world through her eyes. Her words and illusions bridged the gap between the concrete walls of my cell and the vast world beyond. It was a strange dichotomy – the vivid stories painted with her words and her unwavering determination to protect that very world.

Her storytelling went beyond the realm of folklore. She spoke of personal challenges, the hardships she faced, and the sacrifices she made to become a Godlike agent. Her stories were both inspiring and heart-wrenching, and I couldn't help but admire her resilience.

As I listened to Alice's tales, I often found myself yearning for a better understanding of my own abilities. The enigmatic inugami within me remained a source of uncertainty and trepidation. I couldn't explain how or why it activated during the transformation process, brutally taking the lives of the scientists involved.

My mind was a whirlwind of unanswered questions. What triggered the inugami's release? How did it function, and could it be harnessed? These questions gnawed at me, even as Alice's stories provided temporary respite from my self-imposed exile.

As I listened to Alice's stories, a small spark of hope had ignited within me. The weeks spent in solitary confinement were challenging, but they allowed me to reflect and yearn for the moment when I would step outside those prison walls.

That moment finally arrived when Maximus arrived to release me from my cell. My heart raced with anticipation as I followed him through the dimly lit hallways. Alice's presence was reassuring, and her eyes held a flicker of excitement as we made our way to a meeting with Dr. Creed.

Maximus explained the assignment. Dr. Creed had accepted a contract from the government to address a supernatural threat in a foreign country. The public remained blissfully unaware of the existence of the supernatural, and it was our duty to confront these hidden dangers.

The prospect of a real mission stirred both excitement and nervousness within me. I couldn't help but wonder if I was truly ready for such an endeavor. Alice, ever the voice of reason and motivation, explained the nature of our mission and how my role would primarily be one of observation.

"Dr. Creed takes these contracts to ensure that the supernatural remains hidden from the public eye," she said. "We're there to clean up the mess, but you won't be in any immediate danger. You'll have the chance to witness firsthand the world that exists beyond what most people can comprehend."

Maximus chimed in, reassuring me that I was part of a capable team. "We'll make sure you're safe and learn as much as you can from this experience. Our job is to keep the world safe from threats it doesn't even know exist."

With their words of encouragement, my apprehension began to ebb, replaced by a sense of purpose. I was ready to embrace this new challenge, ready to face the unknown and contribute to the greater good. My journey from a troubled young man to a member of the Godlike program had only just begun, and the path ahead was still veiled in mystery, but I was prepared to step boldly into it.

As we gathered for the mission briefing, Dr. Creed's authoritative presence was a calming force in the room. He outlined the details of our assignment in his characteristically enigmatic manner.

"We have received reports of an unusual disturbance in a remote region," he explained. "The locals are experiencing a series of unexplainable phenomena that threaten to expose the supernatural world to the public. It's our duty to investigate, mitigate, and ensure that the truth remains concealed."

Elijah Wayne, who had been relatively quiet until now, spoke up. "I'll be leading this mission. Alice, Cyrus, and Maximus will be my team. Our first objective is to assess the situation, determine the source of these disturbances, and neutralize any supernatural entities causing them."

Alice was her usual composed self, showing no sign of nervousness. "I'll be assisting with reconnaissance and gathering information, and Cyrus will act as our observer."

Maximus, displaying the same stoic confidence he showed in the training arena, added, "Once we identify the threat, I'll take care of eliminating it."

Our roles were clear, and with the objectives set, we prepared to depart. This mission was an opportunity for me to gain a better understanding of the hidden world of the supernatural, to learn from the experiences of my teammates, and to face challenges I had never imagined.

As we readied ourselves for the mission, I couldn't help but feel a sense of anticipation and trepidation. The world of the Godlike program had become my new reality, a realm where the boundaries of what was possible continued to expand, and where the true extent of my potential was yet to be discovered. I was determined to embrace this journey, knowing that every step forward brought me closer to uncovering the secrets of this enigmatic organization and my place within it.

We embarked on a treacherous journey that brought us to the heart of a remote, enigmatic region where the unsettling disturbances had been reported. The path we traversed was fraught with winding trails and dense foliage, leading us deeper into a place shrouded in mystery and foreboding.

The local villagers, their faces etched with fear and confusion, huddled in small clusters, speaking in hushed, uneasy tones. Their distress was palpable, and the eerie events that had recently plagued their lives weighed heavily on their collective psyche. Unexplainable phenomena had disrupted their quiet existence—objects moving of their own accord, lights flickering in an erratic dance, and shadowy figures that materialized and vanished as though pulled from the very fabric of their worst nightmares.

Our arrival in this remote hamlet marked the beginning of an investigation, one that carried the weight of an unknown adversary. The landscape itself seemed to hold secrets and foretell untold mysteries, beckoning us to unearth the source of these disturbances that had thrown the village into turmoil. As we stepped forward, determined to confront the enigma that awaited, I felt the weight of anticipation and uncertainty hanging in the air, mingling with the apprehension of the villagers we were sworn to protect.

DR CREED

As I watched the team's progress on the TV screen monitor, I couldn't help but marvel at their unwavering dedication and loyalty. The operation had brought them to a remote and mysterious region in the heart of the Amazon rainforest, a place where secrets and enigmas were woven into the very fabric of the land.

It was a testament to their trust that they would embark on such a mission without the need for specific details or location. I merely had to convey that an aircraft would transport them to their destination, and they accepted the challenge without question. These were the extraordinary individuals who comprised the Godlike program, and each member brought their unique skills and talents to the table.

Cyrus, in particular, had piqued my interest. He was the newest addition to our team, and this mission had the potential to be a turning point in his journey. I couldn't help but wonder if the Amazon's enigmatic environment would serve as the catalyst to unlock his latent abilities. His potential was a mystery waiting to be unraveled.

As I observed their progress, the Amazon's lush and untamed landscape unfolded before me on the screen. Dense canopies of foliage stretched as far as the eye could see, concealing hidden wonders and dangers alike. This was a place where legends of ancient civilizations, mythical creatures, and supernatural phenomena abounded.

I couldn't help but reflect on my role in this venture. As the enigmatic overseer of the Godlike program, it was my duty to guide these exceptional individuals and provide them with the resources and support they needed. Yet, my true power lay in my knowledge and my own abilities, ones that I had honed over centuries.

The team's mission in the Amazon was one that held the promise of unraveled mysteries, and I knew that their efforts would be instrumental in protecting the world from supernatural threats that remained hidden from public knowledge.

It was with a sense of anticipation and curiosity that I continued to watch their journey, knowing that this was just the beginning of what lay ahead. The Amazon rainforest held many secrets, and I had faith that our team would uncover them, even if it meant confronting the unimaginable.

As I monitored their journey through the Amazon, I couldn't shake the feeling of pride and trepidation. My team was composed of individuals who had honed their unique abilities to levels far beyond the ordinary, and they had proved their mettle in countless missions. Yet, the Amazon held mysteries that had stumped even the most experienced of Godlike agents.

The screen displayed their relentless progress through dense jungles, across treacherous terrain, and through labyrinthine waterways. The villagers they encountered along the way looked upon them with a mix of awe and fear, as though they were walking legends of old. The team's presence had stirred whispers of ancient prophecies and ominous tales of supernatural phenomena.

I observed Cyrus, who had integrated into the team with a mix of determination and humility. While he lacked the supernatural abilities some of the other agents possessed, he more than made up for it with his intelligence, resourcefulness, and a willingness to learn. As he navigated the Amazon's challenges, he seemed eager to prove his worth.

Alice, with her talent for crafting illusions, guided the team through encounters with mysterious entities, dispelling fears and paranoia. Her knowledge of local mythology and folklore played a crucial role in establishing rapport with the villagers and uncovering the heart of their concerns.

Maximus, a powerhouse of telekinetic abilities, provided essential support and protection for the team. He manipulated the environment to their advantage, whether it was creating makeshift bridges, repelling hostile creatures, or manipulating nature's forces to their benefit.

Elijah, with his formidable and mysterious powers, maintained a vigilant presence. He remained a source of unspoken comfort to the team, and his unwavering confidence in the face of the unknown was both inspiring and reassuring.

Our mission was to investigate the series of disturbances that had shaken the region. Unnatural occurrences had sparked fear and chaos among the villagers. Lights flickered mysteriously in the darkness, objects moved seemingly of their own volition, and eerie shadowy figures emerged from the depths of the rainforest, only to vanish into thin air.

As the team delved deeper into the Amazon's heart, they unraveled these mysteries, one by one. They discovered a hidden temple, covered in overgrown vegetation and shrouded in a centuries-old legend. Inside, they found ancient artifacts and inscriptions, revealing the presence of an ancient civilization that worshipped enigmatic entities.

However, the team's exploration was not without its challenges. The Amazon's untamed wilderness tested their limits, and the very land itself seemed to resist their intrusion. They encountered ferocious creatures and faced natural obstacles that demanded the full extent of their abilities and teamwork.

I watched as the team uncovered the heart of the disturbances. It appeared that the ancient temple and its enigmatic artifacts held a link to the supernatural occurrences. The villagers' legends spoke of entities that could manipulate the elements and command the forest itself. The team's findings pointed to a convergence of supernatural energies in this remote region, with potentially dire consequences.

The team returned to their base camp after days of investigation, bringing with them newfound knowledge, but the mysteries of the Amazon's heart still eluded us. It was clear that a deeper and more profound understanding of the supernatural forces at play was required to resolve this conundrum.

I couldn't help but feel a mix of excitement and concern as I observed the team's findings. The Amazon held secrets that could shape the course of our future missions and reveal the true extent of Cyrus's potential. But it also presented dangers and uncertainties that demanded our utmost vigilance.

As I continued to monitor their progress, I knew that our mission in the Amazon was far from over. The supernatural forces at play were powerful and enigmatic, and our journey to unveil their mysteries had only just begun.

CYRUS FINCH

The Amazon journey had been a remarkable and life-changing experience. Alice, Maximus, and Elijah had become not just my comrades but friends on this expedition into the heart of the rainforest. Our close encounters with the villagers, who initially regarded us with a mix of curiosity and apprehension, had evolved into genuine connections. We dined with the locals, learning about their customs and folklore, and they opened their homes to us, their warmth and hospitality reinforcing the feeling of unity that prevailed.

One particularly memorable evening, we were invited for dinner by a local family. Their wooden home nestled amidst the lush greenery was a testament to their resilience in the face of the untamed wilderness. We shared stories, laughter, and food, and I was struck by the simplicity and authenticity of these people's lives. It was a stark contrast to the bustling cityscape I had known, and I felt a deeper connection to the Amazon and its people.

During our exploration, we uncovered the hidden temple, obscured by centuries of overgrowth and legends. The villagers had spoken of an entity that patrolled the Amazon, an enigmatic guardian of the rainforest. As we deciphered the temple's inscriptions and marveled at the ancient artifacts, a complex tapestry of ancient mythology and a supernatural presence emerged. The legends of the guardian began to take shape, and we were left with the ominous question of whether it could be the source of the disturbances.

Upon our return to the base camp, we shared our findings, seeking to unravel the enigma that shrouded the Amazon. Our discussions revolved around deciphering the guardian's nature, and how to confront and, if necessary, subdue it. The plan was to lure it out of hiding, to face it head-on, a formidable task that required meticulous planning and unity.

When the confrontation finally unfolded, the battle against the rainforest creature was a protracted, ferocious struggle that seemed to transcend time. It was as though the entire Amazon rainforest had come to life, contorting and writhing to the creature's malevolent will.

The creature utilized the rainforest itself as its body, and its attacks were relentless, an unending cascade of vegetation and animal life manipulated as weapons. Maximus, with his unrivaled telekinesis, was an unstoppable force, flinging massive tree trunks aside and creating telekinetic barriers to shield us from the onslaught. Alice's illusions danced like specters around the creature, providing distractions, yet its supernatural senses seemed to cut through them.

Elijah, true to his nature, held back his formidable powers, using them only to heal injuries and to lend support. He displayed his incredible agility, leaping between branches and using the vines themselves to launch his attacks.

Our every step was a dance with death, with the creature's roots and vines snapping like serpents at our heels. We scrambled, dodged, and fought through the chaotic battlefield, pushing the creature to its limits.

It retaliated with a wild, unbridled rage. Trees crashed to the ground, crushed by its fury. In its agony, the creature released even more of the Amazon's might upon us. Frenzied flora, now weaponized, was hurled in every direction, seeking to impede our progress.

We were like ants, fighting against a colossal, vengeful titan. Our every move was precarious, and our only recourse was to keep moving, striking when we could.

The creature fought back with an unearthly strength that defied the laws of nature. Its vines lashed out with deadly precision, seeking to choke the life out of us. Yet we persevered, relentlessly pushing forward, our determination unwavering.

As the battle raged on, my sense of awe gave way to profound unease. While my comrades fought with unwavering courage, I remained a passive observer, tormented by my inability to actively participate in the fray. It was frustrating, to say the least, and yet, in their unwavering resolve and unity, I found inspiration.

In a moment of desperation, the creature lashed out, a razor-sharp vine streaking towards Alice with murderous intent. My voice caught in my throat, and I cried out, fearing for her life.

Maximus screamed for me to stop, his words reaching me just as I was about to unleash my command yet I ignored him.

With all the power I could muster, I commanded the creature to die, invoking the dread words that had always come at the direst of moments. A chilling sensation coursed through my veins, and time itself seemed to crawl to a halt.

Suddenly, I found myself seeing through the eyes of a dog, sprinting through the Amazon village. One by one, villagers were consumed by an inexplicable, instantaneous combustion, their bodies reduced to ashes in moments. The sight of their sudden, horrific demise was etched in my memory, a vision of death that filled me with dread.

The time-bending trance released its hold on me, returning me to the present. I watched in astonishment as the rainforest caught fire, the supernatural creature's cries of agony piercing the air. Elijah rushed to Alice's side, his abilities working to heal her wounds, while Maximus dragged us away from the raging inferno to prevent smoke inhalation.

The rainforest was consumed by flames, and the once-invulnerable guardian met its end in the same fiery devastation it had wrought upon the villagers. It was a horrifying, yet cathartic moment, marking the end of a supernatural entity that had haunted the Amazon for centuries.

As we made our way back to the Amazon village, hope in our hearts that we could at least provide some comfort to the survivors, to let them know that they were safe once more. The journey was tense, the memory of the fierce battle still fresh in our minds, but nothing could have prepared us for the horrifying sight that awaited.

The village, once a bustling and thriving community, had been reduced to an eerie silence. Not a soul remained among the huts and pathways. It was as if time had stopped, as if the world had forgotten the existence of this place. And then, the full horror of what had transpired became apparent.

The villagers lay motionless, their bodies charred beyond recognition. They had perished in the same gruesome manner as the rainforest creature, consumed by an invisible force that had rendered them to ashes. The gravity of the devastation weighed heavily upon us all.

Maximus, in a fit of fury and anguish, turned to me, his eyes ablaze with anger. His voice was strained as he demanded, "What have you done, Cyrus?" The accusation was like a dagger to my heart, and I had no answer to give. The consequences of my abilities had spiraled far beyond my control, bringing unfathomable destruction to those we had come to care for.

DR CREED

I stood on the remote airstrip, anticipation and unease building within me. It didn't take long before the aircraft landed, and I watched as Elijah, Alice, Maximus, and Cyrus disembarked, their expressions reflecting a mixture of weariness and relief. They exchanged brief greetings before I intervened.

My tone was stern as I addressed them. "I will debrief you all later," I said to Elijah, Alice, and Maximus, emphasizing the importance of our immediate tasks. Turning to Cyrus, I continued, "You, on the other hand, will have an immediate debrief. Follow me."

I led Cyrus to an empty interrogation room, soldiers flanking us. Taking a seat, I activated my digital pad, preparing to listen to his account of the mission. I instructed him to recount every detail, from the beginning to the devastating end.

As Cyrus spoke, I couldn't help but feel a sense of disappointment, though I concealed it behind my professional façade. His loss of control and the resulting destruction were nothing short of a catastrophe. I knew it was my duty to guide and train our agents, but it seemed that I needed to make Cyrus understand the gravity of his actions.

Once he concluded his story, I couldn't hold back any longer. "Cyrus, you need to learn to control your emotions. I cannot keep cleaning up after you, or there might come a point where you become the very monster we hunt." My words were laced with a sense of urgency and a touch of frustration.

Cyrus tried to defend himself, asserting that they had fulfilled the contract. I countered, "At what cost? You've done more harm than good." The implications of his uncontrolled powers were a burden too heavy for us to bear.

It took some time, but eventually, Cyrus began to grasp the gravity of his actions. He listened as I explained my belief that his abilities required a sacrifice, a price to be paid by those who cared about him to access his godly powers over life and death. I elaborated on the fundamental difference between his power of controlling others with his words and the destructive force he wielded with the inugami, underscoring the weight of the ultimate sacrifice required.

Cyrus absorbed my words, and a realization seemed to wash over him. The somber gravity of his powers and the choices he would have to make weighed on him. The path he had embarked on was a treacherous one, fraught with moral dilemmas and the need to balance the scales between life and death.

I knew that it was essential for him to harness and control his abilities. Our world was one of constant threat, and only the most disciplined and powerful agents could hope to protect it. But there was a limit to the sacrifices we could make for the greater good. In the end, every decision came down to the fine balance between duty and morality.

As I wrapped up the debriefing, I offered Cyrus guidance and encouragement. "You have the potential for greatness, but you must tread carefully. Learn to control your powers, understand the sacrifices involved, and perhaps one day, you will wield them with wisdom."

I was aware that his journey was far from over, but it was my responsibility to ensure that he was prepared for the challenges that lay ahead. The line between being a protector and a harbinger of destruction was a thin one, and it was up to Cyrus to walk it with care.

With the debriefing concluded, I released him with a parting message. "Take time to reflect on what you've learned today, Cyrus. The decisions you make in the future will shape the world we live in."

Cyrus left the interrogation room, perhaps with a newfound sense of purpose and the weight of his responsibilities pressing upon him. For now, he would continue to train and refine his abilities, all while coming to terms with the sacrifices he would be called upon to make in the name of safeguarding our world from the supernatural threats that lurked in the shadows.

The sense of duty weighed heavily on my shoulders as I watched Cyrus leave the interrogation room, his footsteps echoing down the corridor. It was my responsibility to ensure that he was ready for the challenges that lay ahead, but the path he had chosen was treacherous.

I knew that the choices Cyrus would make in the future would have a profound impact on the world we lived in. It was a burden he had to bear, and it was my hope that he would carry it with the wisdom and strength required to protect humanity from the ever-present supernatural threats.

As I contemplated the future, I couldn't help but think about the countless other agents who had walked the same path, each with their own unique abilities and responsibilities. The world was a complex web of secrets and dangers, and the Godlike program was humanity's shield against the unknown.

But with that shield came the weight of sacrifice, a truth that Cyrus had come to understand during our debriefing. He would need to learn how to control his emotions, how to wield his powers with care, and how to strike the delicate balance between duty and morality.

The challenges that lay ahead were formidable, and the battles against supernatural threats unending. But as long as there were agents like Cyrus who were willing to stand against the darkness, there was hope that the world would endure, and that the legacy of the Godlike agents would live on.

My thoughts shifted from the past to the present as I left the interrogation room, heading towards my office. The debriefing had been a somber reminder of the challenges that we faced in our ongoing battle against the supernatural. Each agent brought their own unique set of abilities and struggles, and it was my responsibility to guide them through the perilous journey ahead.

As I settled into my office, I couldn't help but reflect on the countless missions and supernatural threats that had been faced over the years. The world was teeming with hidden dangers, and it was the duty of the Godlike program to protect humanity from the shadows.

My thoughts turned to the current team, led by Elijah, Alice, and Maximus, with Cyrus as the newcomer. Each agent had their strengths and weaknesses, their unique powers and limitations. Together, they were a formidable force, but it was essential to ensure that their abilities were wielded with care and control.

I knew that our work was far from over, and that the supernatural threats lurking in the shadows would continue to challenge us. It was a daunting task, but one that I was determined to face head-on. The fate of the world hung in the balance, and the Godlike agents were our best line of defense.

With that in mind, I began to prepare for the next mission, knowing that the challenges ahead would test our abilities and resolve. The world of the supernatural was a treacherous one, but it was a world that we had sworn to protect.

CYRUS FINCH

As the days turned into weeks, I found myself consumed by a relentless training regimen. Close-quarter combat had become my focus, and the others - Alice, Elijah, and Maximus - were my mentors. They were relentless in pushing me to my limits, and it was the path to mastering my newfound abilities.

We sparred and honed our combat skills, and I marveled at the control and precision of my fellow Godlike agents. Their powers, their command over the supernatural, were nothing short of astonishing. I had a long way to go to reach their level, but I was determined to get there.

It was during these grueling training sessions that I discovered a new facet of my powers - something Dr. Creed referred to as "Absolute Command." This ability granted me the power to impose absolute and irresistible commands upon anything and anyone, even supernatural beings or non-living entities. It was as if I held the strings of reality in my hands, molding the world around me with my intentions and commands.

Learning to harness this newfound power was both exhilarating and exhausting. The mere act of using it drained me of energy, leaving me physically and mentally fatigued. But the potential it offered was boundless. I could grant myself or others any power or ability I wished, simply by uttering a command. The challenge lay in the intent behind the command, ensuring that it was both clear and unwavering.

I practiced relentlessly, experimenting with my newfound abilities, bending reality to my will. With a single word or gesture, I could impose complex commands, reshaping the world in accordance with my intentions. It was awe-inspiring and daunting, knowing that this power rested in my hands.

But it wasn't without its drawbacks. Using Absolute Command was a double-edged sword. The more potent the command, the greater the energy it drained from me. It was as if each command exacted a toll on my very soul. I quickly learned that moderation was key, and that recklessness could leave me weakened and vulnerable.

In contrast, I had the Inugami, a supernatural entity at my disposal, obedient to my will. It required no immense expenditure of energy and using it to carry out my commands felt more natural. However, it came with a cost - a steep and harrowing one. To employ the Inugami's abilities, a sacrifice had to be made. It was a grim reminder that power came at a price, and I had to be judicious in my choices.

As the weeks turned into months, I trained, learned, and grew stronger. My newfound abilities were evolving, and the line between my power over life and death and my control over others was blurring. It was a delicate balance to strike, one that I had yet to master fully.

The path to becoming a true Godlike agent was arduous, filled with challenges, sacrifices, and relentless training. But the desire to protect the world from supernatural threats was a powerful driving force. I was committed to the cause, no matter the price.

In the shadowy world of the Godlike program, we faced the unknown, walked on the precipice of power and danger. And as I pushed myself further each day, I couldn't help but wonder how far I was willing to go, and what sacrifices I might be called upon to make in the name of safeguarding humanity from the supernatural lurking in the shadows.

My journey to harness and master my abilities continued, and every day brought new challenges and revelations. It was a path marked by growth and struggle, and I was committed to making the most of the unique powers bestowed upon me.

As I trained alongside Alice, Elijah, and Maximus, I felt a growing camaraderie among us. They were my mentors, my companions, and my friends, and together we formed a formidable team. Each day was an opportunity to learn from their wisdom and experience, and they never hesitated to push me to my limits.

With the passage of time, my control over Absolute Command became more refined. I learned to wield it with precision, shaping reality to my will. This ability was both a gift and a responsibility, and I was determined to use it wisely.

Yet, even as I honed my powers, the sacrifice involved in using the Inugami weighed heavily on my conscience. I had witnessed firsthand the grim price it extracted, and I knew that every decision had consequences. The line between wielding these abilities for the greater good and succumbing to their darker aspects was a fine one, and I was determined not to cross it.

Our training sessions expanded to include scenarios where we faced formidable supernatural threats. These simulations helped prepare us for the unpredictable nature of our work. The world was filled with unknown dangers, and we were the line of defense against them.

Amidst the trials and tribulations, I was reminded of Dr. Creed's words about controlling my emotions. The power I held required a deep understanding of myself and an unwavering sense of discipline. I was determined to heed his advice and not become a liability to the team.

In the world of the Godlike program, every decision and every action carried weight. We were tasked with protecting humanity from the shadows, safeguarding it from supernatural threats that lurked beyond the veil of ordinary perception. It was a responsibility we shouldered with unwavering dedication.

As I continued my training and the bond among my mentors and me grew stronger, I couldn't help but feel a sense of purpose. The power I possessed was a double-edged sword, and I was committed to wielding it with the wisdom it demanded.

The path to becoming a true Godlike agent was a journey filled with uncertainty and danger. But I embraced the challenges and the sacrifices, for I had become a guardian against the supernatural forces that threatened our world. In this shadowy realm, I would do whatever it took to protect humanity, no matter the cost.

Each day was a test of my willpower and abilities. Training with Alice, Elijah, and Maximus had become both exhilarating and daunting. The bond among us deepened as we worked tirelessly to prepare for the supernatural threats that lurked in the shadows.

Absolute Command was a power that I had to wield with caution and precision. I practiced it extensively, learning to impose commands with clarity and purpose. With each use, I felt the drain on my energy, a reminder of the immense responsibility that came with such authority. My commands could be a force for good, but I had to be vigilant to avoid letting them spiral out of control.

The Inugami, on the other hand, was my supernatural ally. It responded to my commands without sapping my energy, providing a unique advantage. However, I couldn't forget the price it exacted. Sacrifices were made, and I was constantly reminded of the cost of wielding its power.

I often found myself in deep contemplation, reflecting on the fine line I walked between life and death, control and chaos. The question of what it meant to be a Godlike agent weighed heavily on me. The sacrifices we made for the greater good, the risks we undertook, all became part of the journey.

With each day, I grew more proficient in using my powers. I honed my abilities, finding the synergy between my power over life and death and my influence over others. It was a delicate balance, a dance that required constant practice and vigilance.

The training pit became a battleground of powers, and Maximus and I stood ready to test our abilities. The battle between Maximus and me erupted with a series of initial blows. Maximus wielded his formidable telekinetic abilities, his attacks precise and relentless, and I did my best to evade his onslaught. I was acutely aware of the energy drain that would accompany using my Absolute Command and decided to hold it in reserve for a crucial moment.

As Maximus gradually cornered me, the pressing need for a game-changing move became apparent. At that moment, I uttered a powerful command to myself, "Grant me enhanced strength, unparalleled speed, and reflexes beyond human limits," invoking my Absolute Command. A surge of power coursed through me, and my physical attributes ascended to an astonishing degree.

With this newfound strength and agility, I nimbly danced around Maximus, delivering a barrage of rapid strikes and powerful combos. His initial surprise soon transformed into a more serious and determined demeanor as I skillfully maintained the upper hand in our lengthy and intense battle.

However, Maximus was not one to be outdone. In the midst of our ongoing combat, he experienced a transformation, an unlocking of his telekinetic abilities into the profound realm of Omnikinesis. This development shifted the dynamics of our battle as he gained the power to manipulate matter, controlling the environment to his advantage.

The battle between Maximus and me continued to escalate in both intensity and complexity as he harnessed his newly unlocked Omni Kinetic abilities. His mastery over matter shifted the very nature of our combat, turning the battleground into a chaotic maelstrom of constantly shifting terrains and an array of manipulated objects.

With his godlike powers, Maximus could now control the environment with unparalleled precision. Chunks of the ground were hurled toward me, each propelled with tremendous force. The earth itself became a weapon in his hands.

Utilizing my enhanced agility and speed, I deftly leaped from one fragment of the ground to another, a dance of evasion and aggression. As I closed the distance between us, I delivered a powerful blow that broke through Maximus's telekinetic armor, a crushing hit that seriously injured him for the first time in our arduous battle.

Maximus, despite his injury, remained unyielding and resolute. With his newfound abilities, the battlefield continued to shift, morph, and transform, putting my adaptability and combat skills to the test. It was a long and grueling struggle, with each of us pushing our limits to the extreme.

My energy reserves began to wane, and with each passing moment, the temptation to call upon my Inugami, Chase, to assist me grew stronger. However, with Elijah's penetrating gaze fixed upon me, the uncertainty of whether he could read my intentions kept me from making that final, desperate move.

In the end, with a heavy heart and a sense of my limitations, I made the difficult decision to concede the match. The implications of wielding my powers, the sacrifices involved, and the ethical dilemmas associated with it had never been more apparent.

DR CREED

I watched the intense battle between Cyrus and Maximus from within the crowd of spectators, the raw power and fierce determination displayed by both combatants leaving a strong impression. I leaned toward Alice, who stood beside me, and remarked on Cyrus's impressive abilities.

Alice nodded, her expression a mixture of pride and concern. "The training is going great, but I can't shake the feeling that Cyrus is becoming more machine than man, thanks to the Godlike Project."

I considered her words, knowing that the Godlike Project had a tendency to strip away emotions and replace them with enhanced abilities. "Well, we're building weapons, not friends," I replied, a sense of pragmatism in my tone. I decided to share a piece of information I had been holding back. "In fact, I chose Cyrus because I knew he had sociopathic tendencies."

Alice's eyes widened in surprise, but she didn't question my choice. She understood the necessity of selecting agents who could carry out difficult missions without the burden of emotions.

With the fight concluded and my agents in need of rest, I decided to reveal the details of their upcoming mission. "Cyrus and Maximus need to get some rest. You'll leaving in twenty-four hours." I then gestured for Alice to follow me. "Come with me. Elijah and I will brief you on the mission."

After the remarkable fight, Alice and I made our way to my office, and I couldn't help but feel a sense of trepidation about the upcoming mission. It was essential that our team was prepared and in the right state of mind. However, I knew we couldn't afford to be lenient when it came to the responsibilities and the moral dilemmas we faced.

We entered my office to find Elijah already waiting for us. Without much ado, we settled in, and I began the mission debrief. "As I was telling Alice, we'll be heading to Paris for an investigation. There's a warehouse dock that has seen a disturbing number of missing persons cases. The French government initially contracted this mission to G.O.D., but it got passed down to us."

Alice, always diligent and cautious, raised her concern once more. "Dr. Creed, are you certain that Cyrus is ready for fieldwork? I don't want his recent experiences to cloud his judgment or affect the mission."

Elijah, with his intense focus and conviction, spoke up. "I have been training Cyrus personally, and I believe he is ready. He has shown remarkable improvement both in his abilities and his mental strength. But let me make this clear, Dr. Creed: if Cyrus ever crosses the line and poses a threat to our mission or the safety of our team, I will not hesitate to eliminate him myself."

I nodded in acknowledgment. It was a heavy burden to carry, but it was the reality of the world we live in. "Thank you, Elijah. It's crucial that we maintain the balance between our duty and morality in this line of work. We'll trust that Cyrus is ready and that he has learned from his past experiences. Our mission is to ensure its success."

I continued to lay out the mission details, explaining that the disappearances seemed to follow a pattern closely associated with vampires. The fact that the French government believed a notorious French vampire involved in dealings with Moros Noctis was operating at the docks added a layer of urgency to our mission. As I emphasized, we needed this vampire alive for questioning, as it could lead us to more critical information.

"The time of day these people are vanishing, and the patterns suggest it's a vampire," I concluded. "Our primary target is this French vampire connected to Moros Noctis. It's crucial that we bring him in alive. However, we should be prepared for potential conflicts with his coven or others involved."

Elijah and Alice listened intently, and the gravity of our mission was palpable in the room. We all knew the risks and challenges that lay ahead, but our determination to protect the world from the supernatural threats gave us the resolve to face whatever came our way.

Our preparations continued as we gathered the necessary supplies, reviewed intelligence reports, and finalized our travel arrangements. There was an air of quiet anticipation that accompanied our every move, a shared understanding that our mission would take us into the heart of danger.

I observed Cyrus's absence closely. His recent battle had demonstrated his abilities, but it was his readiness to face the unknown that intrigued me. He was a wildcard, and our collective trust in him was founded on his potential and his capacity to control his powers.

In the coming hours, they would board a plane bound for Paris, a city known for its beauty and history but also a place where darkness lurked in the underbelly of the world. It was a place where the supernatural coexisted with the mundane, and where they, as godlike agents, were the guardians against the malevolent forces that threatened humanity.

As we made our way to the airport, I couldn't help but reflect on the responsibility that rested on our shoulders. The fate of the missing souls, the French vampire, and the safety of the world rested with us. The shadows of the unknown awaited, and we would soon step into the darkness with unwavering resolve, prepared to confront the supernatural threats that Paris held.

The journey had just begun, and our destinies were intertwined with the secrets and dangers that lay hidden within the warehouse docks of the City of Light.

As I watched Alice, Cyrus, Maximus, and Elijah board the private luxury plane that would take them to Paris, a sense of unease settled in the pit of my stomach. They were heading into the unknown, facing the supernatural threats that plagued the world. I knew that their determination and abilities would serve them well, but I couldn't help but worry for their safety.

With a heavy heart, I turned away from the departing plane and made my way back to the car. The driver was waiting, and we began the journey back to the godlike compound. The world outside sped by in a blur, and I couldn't help but feel a sense of foreboding.

As we neared the compound, a rising plume of smoke came into view, and my heart sank. The compound had been reduced to smoldering ruins, and the devastation was beyond comprehension. All our AI defenses, gunners, turrets, everything had been systematically destroyed. The charred remains of countless godlike project members littered the area, and it was a grim testament to the ruthlessness of our assailants.

Amidst the destruction, I saw one figure standing in the center of the chaos, a lone finger raised in a mocking gesture. Moros Noctis, the very embodiment of malevolence and darkness. His smile sent a shiver down my spine as he taunted me with his presence.

"You're looking for me?" he asked with a twisted grin.

CYRUS FINCH

Arriving in France, we proceeded to our respective hotels, each registered under various aliases. I had the advantage of fluency in French, so I took on most of the communication duties. Maximus noted that he had never stayed in such a luxurious establishment, and it was clear that the opulence of the place left an impression on him.

I couldn't help but smile at his awe. "I've been to this hotel multiple times," I explained, "and I'm quite familiar with its layout from my youth."

Alice, always full of surprises, began chatting with the bellhop in fluent French. The rest of us exchanged puzzled glances, unsure of how she had suddenly become so proficient.

"I didn't know you could speak French," I remarked, intrigued.

Alice, ever the enigma, revealed her secret. "I use audio illusions on myself," she confessed. "It's a handy skill for someone in our line of work. I can make myself understand and speak different languages when the need arises."

Her ability to adapt so quickly never ceased to amaze me, and it was a reminder of how unique and versatile each member of our team truly was.

In our hotel rooms, we gathered to hash out our plan of action. This particular hotel was chosen strategically for its proximity to the point of interest: the docks, where many of the recent tourists had mysteriously vanished.

We unpacked our gear and sat down to discuss our strategy. Elijah, as always, took the lead and outlined our mission. Our first objective was to identify the supernatural creature involved. Once we had that information, we would move forward with a plan to neutralize it and, if necessary, deal with any potential nest of these creatures.

As we talked through the details, I couldn't shake a growing sense of unease. We were venturing into the unknown, confronting dangers that were difficult to predict. But as a team, we were determined to face the supernatural threat lurking in the shadows and bring an end to the mysterious disappearances that had plagued the city.

Elijah's plan was both brilliant and unsettling. He had deduced that the mysterious creature might be a vampire, and to test this theory, he intended to use Alice as bait.

The idea didn't sit well with me, and I voiced my concerns, but Elijah quickly silenced me so he could explain the full plan. I couldn't deny that his plan was effective and thorough, given his expertise in hunting supernatural creatures and his deep understanding of psychological warfare.

Late at night, in the elegant bar of the hotel, Alice donned a stunning red dress and took on her role as the bait. She moved with grace, casting sensory illusions that emitted the enticing smell of potent blood as she passed by each person in the bar. Cyrus, Maximus, and I hid in different corners of the establishment, our eyes locked on Alice as she navigated through the unsuspecting patrons. Alice was an espionage expert, and this mission was far from her first.

As she moved among the people, a few men finally reacted to the illusion, their eyes revealing the telltale signs of being a vampire. Veins bulged, and fangs made brief appearances. One man, in particular, couldn't resist the allure of the illusion, and he quickly approached Alice, offering to buy her a drink. The trap was set, and we waited in tense anticipation to see how the vampire would respond to our bait.

The vampire's approach was cautious but filled with a hunger that he couldn't fully suppress. He engaged Alice in conversation, skillfully hiding his true nature behind a facade of charm and interest. As they talked, the others in the bar seemed oblivious to the unfolding drama.

Alice played her role expertly, drawing the vampire in further, all while maintaining the sensory illusion. Her composure was unwavering as the tension in the room rose. The three of us watched from our hidden positions, ready to spring into action at a moment's notice.

Elijah's plan hinged on observing the vampire's reactions, assessing his intent, and determining if there were other supernatural creatures accompanying him. It was a delicate dance of strategy and deception, one that required precision and patience.

The vampire's persistence in maintaining his cover made us wonder if he was genuinely alone or if he was part of a larger network of supernatural beings. We knew that our next steps would be crucial in unveiling the truth behind the mysterious disappearances in this city, and it all hinged on how the vampire would respond to Alice's tempting illusion.

Our tense vigil continued in the dimly lit bar, the minutes stretching like hours as Alice skillfully manipulated the vampire, coaxing information and gauging his reactions. The entire operation hung in a precarious balance.

Elijah, Maximus, and I remained hidden, our senses heightened and focused on every nuance of the encounter. The vampire's careful facade was slipping, revealing fleeting glimpses of his true nature.

Suddenly, as the conversation progressed, the atmosphere in the bar shifted. Other patrons seemed to become aware that something unusual was happening, their eyes shifting towards our corner, where the three of us were concealed.

The vampire's fangs became more pronounced, and he made a subtle move that hinted at his intent. It was the moment we had been waiting for. With a discreet signal from Elijah, we sprang into action.

Elijah used his supernatural speed to close the distance between him and the vampire in the blink of an eye. Maximus unleashed a surge of telekinetic force, creating a barrier between the vampires and the rest of the bar, sealing them off from the world.

In the relentless pulse of the club, the air thickened with anticipation as the vampire's true nature was laid bare. With my absolute command over the ethereal, the impending confrontation took on a visceral edge—a standoff between our team and a supernatural adversary, the stakes dripping with the bloodlust of the night.

I extended my hands, fingers curling with the weight of absolute authority. The dance began as I commanded shadows to ensnare the vampires, a macabre waltz of dominance. Maximus, with raw Omni kinetic force, engaged the undead in a kinetic tango, his hands a blur deflecting their attacks with ruthless precision.

Elijah, an enigma bathed in a mystic aura, unleashed his powers through primal gestures. Radiant waves surged from his fingertips, repelling the vampires in a violent ballet of unseen forces. Alice, a mistress of illusions, wove nightmare scenarios with the mere movement of her hands, rendering the undead disoriented and vulnerable.

As the confrontation escalated, the vampires closed in, and the melee became intimate. My hands, charged with absolute command, became instruments of ethereal cruelty, tearing through the undead with a commanding brutality. Maximus engaged in hand-to-hand combat, his Omni kinetic force enhancing every strike as he dismantled the undead assailants.

Elijah's hands conducted an unseen symphony of devastation, manipulating the very fabric of reality to crush and repel our foes. Alice's hands weaved illusions that tore through the vampires' perceptions, making the fight a psychological nightmare in addition to a physical one.

In the heart of the chaos, the vampire leader emerged. His fangs bared, he lunged with predatory aggression. My hands commanded the shadows to coil around him, immobilizing him in a vice-like grip. Maximus, Elijah, and Alice converged, each using their hands to deliver decisive blows that left the leader broken and defeated.

The aftermath revealed a blood-soaked tableau—the club's floor a canvas of crimson testament to the personal nature of our battle. One vampire remained, cowed and broken. As we approached, a glimmer of humanity flickered in its eyes, a stark reminder that even in the blood-stained dance of the supernatural, there were casualties not born of malice but of dark circumstance.

The vampire guiding us to the warehouse was captivating, his aura steeped in the weight of centuries of existence. He spoke in hushed tones with a charming French accent, painting a vivid picture of the vampire lord, Sébastien Renforcé, who had ruled for millennia with near-mythical power.

The journey led us through a labyrinth of darkened alleys and concealed passages, deep into the heart of the city. The warehouse appeared, its foreboding presence hinting at the secrets concealed within. Our vampire informant, however, held the key to a hidden entrance, ensuring our covert entry into the warehouse.

As we entered, a shiver of anticipation ran down my spine, the unknown awaiting us inside the warehouse filling the air with tension. Yet, as our guide began to reveal the location of Sébastien Renforcé, the very shadows came alive with hissing whispers and the sound of approaching footsteps.

Without warning, the vampires launched a sudden ambush, their movements and strategy precise and deadly. The treacherous intent of our guide was laid bare, having led us into this perilous trap. Swiftly, Elijah responded with brutal efficiency, his supernatural speed and strength leaving him unrivaled.

In a flash, he seized our treacherous informant, tearing out his heart with ruthless precision. As the lifeless body fell, Elijah turned his icy gaze toward the remaining attackers, his expression devoid of mercy. "Oh. Was he a friend of yours?" he quipped; his words laden with chilling irony.

The room goes quiet, the eerie silence settling like a heavy shroud, right before the vampires unleash their ferocious counterattack. In that suspended moment, anticipation hangs thick in the air, our collective breaths hanging in the balance as we prepare for the impending clash.

Suddenly, the vampires surge forward, a relentless tide of supernatural foes converging upon us with savage determination. Alice, in her unparalleled mastery of absolute illusion, unleashes the full might of her powers. The illusions she crafts become a living tapestry, bringing gods from mythology to life to fight by our side. It's a breathtaking display of her abilities, a vivid manifestation of ancient deities standing shoulder to shoulder with modern-day warriors.

As the illusions come to life, gods like Zeus, Prometheus, Ra, Odin, and Loki materialize to join the fray. The room transforms into a battlefield of epic proportions, where mortal and immortal forces collide in a spectacle that transcends the boundaries of reality. The once-confident vampires falter in the face of this divine intervention, their predatory advance disrupted by the unexpected appearance of mythical beings.

In the midst of this supernatural maelstrom, I, Cyrus, embrace the might of absolute command. Muscles ripple as I surge forward with godlike strength, each step landing like a battering ram. Delving deep within myself, I unlock the ability of sun fire, searing the vampire's flesh with attacks marked by unparalleled speed and precision.

The vampire onslaught proves relentless, a coordinated and synchronized force that pushes us to the brink. Undeterred, we meet their charge head-on, refusing to relent in the face of their relentless assault. The gods from mythology, summoned by Alice's illusions, fight alongside us with otherworldly prowess, creating a harmonious blend of mortal and immortal forces.

As the battle rages on, the illusions Alice sustains require an immense amount of energy. Yet, she persists, determined to hold the line against the vampire onslaught. The gods she conjured clash with the vampires in a display of supernatural might, their ancient powers unleashed in a symphony of destruction.

The Vampire Lord Sébastien Renforcé, observing from the periphery, watches with an unreadable expression. The gods and vampires clash with a ferocity that transcends the supernatural realm, and the outcome of this struggle will not only determine the success of our mission but also reveal the true extent of the threats that lurk in the shadows.

Amidst the chaos, Elijah, Maximus, and I continue our relentless assault, our abilities combining with the divine entities summoned by Alice to create a seamless blend of mortal and immortal might. The room echoes with the clash of steel, the crackle of supernatural energies, and the roars of ancient gods battling creatures of the night. In this intricate dance of combat, the boundaries between reality and myth blur, creating a battleground where the fate of our mission hangs in the balance.

In the midst of the chaotic confrontation, Sebastian, the formidable vampire lord, proved to be a force beyond any we had faced before. His strength eclipsed that of the vampires combined, catching us off guard as he swiftly knocked Maximus, Alice, Elijah, and me to the side. The ensuing four-on-one battle unfolded in a frenetic flurry of blows, but Sebastian effortlessly dodged every strike, countering with a brutal efficiency that sent us flying.

While Sebastian focused on us, Alice utilized her illusionary gods to eradicate the remaining vampires. Maximus, harnessing his omni kinetic abilities, hurled chunks of the ground toward the vampire lord. Leaping from each piece, I mirrored the agility I had demonstrated against Maximus in our training match, closing the distance with Sebastian. Alice followed closely behind, her every move synchronized with our attack.

Maximus heightened the velocity of the flying rocks, creating a distraction for Sebastian. Seizing the opportunity, Elijah opened a portal for Alice and me, bringing us behind the vampire lord. Emerging from the portal, I delivered a powerful blow to the back of Sebastian's head, while Alice unleashed a forceful kick. The vampire lord was propelled into the chunks of rocks Maximus had sent his way, and Elijah brought them to life.

The collision into the sentient rocks disoriented Sebastian, turning the encounter into a nightmarish ordeal for him. The rocks wrapped their hands around him, biting into his flesh with ragged rock teeth. Maximus took control, manipulating the sentient rocks to send the vampire lord flying in different directions, slamming him into the remaining vampires with such force that they were atomized. Elijah, with a snap of his fingers, triggered the explosion of the sentient rocks, propelling Sebastian downward.

Angry, bruised, and dusting himself off, Sebastian flaunted his frustration. This was the first time he had been hurt since becoming a vampire lord, and disrespect was not something he took lightly. Speaking in a French accent, he explained that he had wiped out entire bloodlines for less. As he transformed into a vampire lordship, growing leathery bat wings, sharper fangs, and claws, Sebastian launched a relentless attack with all his might.

Forced to take the battle seriously, we faced a deadlier adversary than all the vampires combined. Sebastian fought with eons of experience and a primal desire to kill and prey on his victims. In the midst of the escalating battle, I couldn't help but ponder that if Godlike wanted efficient killers, perhaps Dr. Creed should have indeed gone with vampires. As the fight raged on, Sebastian expertly kept up with four trained Godlike agents, turning the confrontation into a relentless dance of predator and prey.

Sebastian, now transformed into a formidable vampire lord, continued to put up a relentless fight against our coordinated efforts. His bat wings slashed through the air with deadly precision, and his fangs and claws became even more formidable with each passing moment. The dance of battle unfolded in a chaotic symphony, the clash of supernatural forces echoing through the darkened warehouse.

As I engaged Sebastian in close combat, his movements were a blur of lethal strikes and evasions. Maximus utilized his omni kinetic abilities to manipulate the environment, sending objects hurtling toward Sebastian to create openings. Elijah's portals allowed for strategic repositioning, ensuring we maintained an element of surprise in our attacks. Meanwhile, Alice masterfully orchestrated her illusionary gods, bringing forth powerful entities from mythology to aid us in the struggle.

Sebastian, however, was not easily overpowered. His experience as a vampire lord showcased an intimate understanding of combat, and his instincts were honed over centuries. Despite our combined efforts, he skillfully deflected blows and retaliated with a relentless ferocity that kept us on the defensive.

The intensity of the battle heightened as Sebastian unleashed his newfound powers, employing dark sorcery to manipulate shadows and summoning creatures of the night to join the fray. The odds seemed increasingly stacked against us, and it became clear that subduing Sebastian without resorting to lethal force would be a formidable challenge.

In a moment of strategic brilliance, Alice devised a plan to incapacitate Sebastian without causing permanent harm. With a focused concentration, she wove a potent illusion around the vampire lord. In this illusion, Sebastian found himself trapped in a never-ending cycle of deprivation, where he experienced the torment of being drained of blood repeatedly. The illusion played out in excruciating detail, exploiting the psychological vulnerabilities of a creature so accustomed to preying on others.

As the illusory thirst tormented Sebastian, it weakened his resolve and diverted his attention. This created the opening we needed to coordinate our efforts. Maximus seized control of the environment, constraining Sebastian's movements with telekinetic force. Elijah manipulated shadows to further disorient the vampire lord, while I delivered precise strikes to weaken his physical defenses.

The combined assault reached its climax as Alice's illusion took full effect. Sebastian, ensnared by the illusionary nightmare, began to lose coherence in the physical realm. His resistance waned, allowing us to subdue him without inflicting fatal injuries. The battle-weary vampire lord, caught in the illusionary web of his deepest fears, was left incapacitated, a testament to the power of our coordinated efforts and Alice's ingenious use of her abilities.

As the adrenaline of the battle began to subside, we stood over the defeated Sebastian, contemplating the challenges that lay ahead in the world of supernatural threats. The warehouse, once filled with chaos, now echoed with the quiet aftermath of our victory – a victory that, against all odds, spared the life of the formidable vampire lord.

DR CREED

In the midst of the chaotic aftermath, Moros Noctis stood with a sinister grin, his taunting presence a challenge to all who dared oppose him. As the embodiment of malevolence and darkness, his malevolent aura cast a pall over the destruction surrounding us. Moros' twisted words echoed through the wreckage, sending an unsettling shiver down my spine.

"You're looking for me?" he mocked, a single finger raised in a gesture that conveyed both arrogance and contempt. The confrontation was inevitable, and I squared my shoulders, preparing for the impending clash.

The battle commenced with Moros Noctis, reveling in his divine shadow abilities, launching bolts of malevolent energy toward me. Swiftly evading his attacks, I dodged and weaved through the onslaught, desperately attempting to stay one step ahead of the relentless assault. Moros, sensing my evasion, intensified the barrage, each shadow bolt carrying the weight of divine malice.

Despite my efforts, Moros had pushed me to my limits, forcing me to shed the façade of Dr. Creed, the unassuming doctor. It was time to reveal the true extent of my power, the ancient kitsune abilities that surpassed the ordinary realm. Channeling the elements—fire, wind, lightning, time, music, earth, shadow, and soul—I unleashed a torrent of energy in response.

The battlefield became a swirling dance of elemental forces as divine shadows clashed with the formidable powers of a kitsune. Yet, Moros' strength, amplified by his connection to divine fury, proved overwhelming. The relentless assault left me on the defensive, my movements dictated by the malevolent whims of my adversary.

Moros played with me like a puppet, a grim reminder of the vast power he wielded. His divine shadows twisted and contorted, creating an intricate web that ensnared me. Each attempt to counter or retaliate was met with an unyielding force that pushed me further into a defensive stance.

As I zipped around the battlefield, avoiding Moros' attacks, I couldn't shake the realization that I was dancing on the edge of defeat. His power, fueled by nefarious forces beyond mortal comprehension, pressed relentlessly against the limits of my kitsune abilities.

Moros' laughter echoed through the chaos, a maddening sound that taunted my every move. The battle had become a relentless struggle for survival, a clash of powers that transcended the ordinary boundaries of the mortal and supernatural realms. Yet, in the face of overwhelming odds, I fought on, determined to confront the embodiment of darkness and protect the fragile balance that held our world together.

The battlefield crackled with the clash of elemental forces, a symphony of power that reverberated through the chaotic arena. Moros Noctis, the embodiment of malevolence, and I, Dr. Creed, a kitsune harnessing the elemental might within, engaged in a relentless dance of shadows and flames.

In the heart of the ethereal battleground, I delved deep into the reservoirs of my kitsune essence, drawing forth the very soul of fire. Flames erupted around me, an infernal symphony that roared with the unrestrained fury of elemental power. The scorching tongues of fire, imbued with ancient magic, danced in chaotic harmony as if they possessed a life of their own.

Moros, the malevolent force opposing me, met my fiery onslaught with a counter that resonated with the essence of divine shadow. His outstretched hands became conduits for a shadowy force that emerged like an insatiable void, a force that seemed to feed on the very essence of light itself. The stark contrast between the blazing fire and the devouring shadows created a mesmerizing tableau, an otherworldly battlefield where the boundaries between creation and malevolence blurred.

As I manipulated the elemental forces, the flames surged with newfound vigor, twisting and coiling in intricate patterns. The inferno took on ethereal shapes—spiraling phoenixes, writhing serpents, and mythical beasts formed from the searing heat. They became my fiery allies, extensions of my will in the cosmic tapestry we wove.

Moros, however, remained an unwavering shadow in the midst of the inferno. His divine shadow swirled around him like an ever-hungry serpent, a force that sought to extinguish the very flames that sought to defy it. The cosmic dance between fire and shadow unfolded, each movement a calculated step in the intricate ballet of power.

The battlefield became a canvas, painted with strokes of light and darkness, an evolving masterpiece that echoed with the clash of elemental might. Fire and shadow intertwined, creating an interplay of hues that transcended mortal comprehension. The very air crackled with the volatile energy born from the collision of opposing forces.

With a gesture, Moros intensified the divine shadow, causing it to surge forward with a predatory hunger. The flames responded in kind, roaring in defiance as if to resist the encroaching darkness. It was a cosmic tug-of-war, a struggle that epitomized the eternal conflict between creation and malevolence.

The flames, fueled by my kitsune essence, manifested in unprecedented forms. Firestorms swept across the battleground, and tendrils of ethereal flame reached out like spectral hands, eager to consume all in their path. Moros, undeterred, manipulated his divine shadow with preternatural finesse, weaving a defensive shroud that defied the relentless assault.

In the midst of the elemental chaos, I channeled the essence of wind to amplify the flames. Whirlwinds of searing heat spiraled around me, creating a vortex that intensified the inferno's destructive power. The very fabric of the battlefield quivered as the elemental forces clashed, an epic struggle that transcended the boundaries of mortal understanding.

The dance between fire and shadow reached its zenith, a crescendo of power that reverberated through the cosmic tapestry. The forces clashed with unparalleled intensity, each seeking dominion over the other. The very foundation of the battlefield trembled under the strain of elemental conflict, and the air crackled with an otherworldly energy.

As the clash continued, the boundary between creation and malevolence blurred further, and the very essence of the battlefield became a testament to the eternal struggle between opposing forces. The cosmic ballet unfolded, a spectacle that defied the limitations of the mortal realm, and in that moment, the destiny of the ethereal clash hung in precarious balance.

Moros, fueled by his nogitsune, unleashed relentless barrages of divine shadow bolts. Each strike was calculated, a malevolent dance that sought to corner me within the ethereal onslaught. I navigated the tempest with nimble agility, leaving trails of flickering shadows in my wake.

The battlefield became a canvas for our clash, an intricate tapestry woven with fire and shadow. My Kitsune abilities manifested in rapid succession—whirlwinds of wind, crackling bolts of lightning, echoes of music that resonated with ancient power, and the shaping of the very earth beneath us. Each elemental force responded to my command, a testament to the centuries of mastery embedded within my kitsune essence.

Yet, Moros proved to be a relentless adversary, deftly countering my every move. His divine shadow seemed to anticipate my elemental onslaught, a force that adapted and resisted like a sentient being. The struggle intensified, the air thick with the scent of scorched shadows and the resonant echoes of elemental clashes.

In a surge of elemental power, I summoned the essence of time, manipulating its flow to momentarily freeze Moros in his malevolent tracks. It was a brief respite, a fraction of a second, but it allowed me to unleash a torrent of elemental attacks. Fire roared, wind howled, and lightning crackled in a crescendo of power.

Moros, however, emerged from the temporal manipulation unscathed, his grin twisted with amusement. Divine shadow flowed around him, a protective cloak that seemed impervious to the elemental onslaught. The battlefield tilted in his favor, the cosmic dance favoring malevolence.

As I surveyed the relentless storm of divine shadow, a surge of determination fueled my Kitsune abilities. I channeled the very essence of my being into a final, desperate effort. A fusion of elemental forces manifested—a symphony of fire, wind, lightning, and shadows converging into a dazzling display of power.

The clash reached its zenith, the battlefield ablaze with elemental fury. For a fleeting moment, it seemed as though the scales might tip in my favor. Yet, Moros, the embodiment of malevolence, stood resolute. His divine shadow expanded, eclipsing the kaleidoscope of elemental might with an engulfing darkness.

In the ensuing chaos, Moros exploited a vulnerability in my elemental defenses. With a malevolent grin, he unleashed a surge of divine shadow that engulfed me, casting a suffocating veil over my elemental prowess. The symphony of power became a dissonant dirge, and I found myself ensnared within the shadows.

Moros' twisted laughter echoed through the shadows as he reveled in his triumph. The battlefield, once vibrant with elemental clashes, fell into an oppressive silence. My consciousness struggled against the encroaching darkness, and I braced for the inevitable.

Enveloped by the encroaching shadows, Moros Noctis materialized from the dissipating cosmic maelstrom, his grin stretching with sadistic delight. The once tumultuous battlefield, now bereft of the clash of elemental powers, bore silent testimony to his triumph. As the shadows consumed my vision, the haunting echoes of

Moros' malevolent laughter reverberated through the abyss, marking the somber conclusion of the cosmic conflict.

CYRUS FINCH

The room echoed with an air of tension as we surrounded Sebastian, the defeated vampire lord. The aftermath of the battle still lingered, the scent of burnt shadows and lingering illusions mixing in the air. Alice, Elijah, and Maximus stood ready, their expressions unwavering masks of determination.

Alice, the mistress of illusions, took the lead. Her eyes glowed with an otherworldly intensity as she delved into the recesses of Sebastian's mind, preparing to unleash the torment that awaited him. I watched, a mixture of fascination and trepidation settling in my gut. Alice began weaving her illusions, creating a dreamscape that would blur the lines between reality and the nightmarish fantasies of the vampire lord.

Sebastian, despite his defiant exterior, couldn't escape the clutches of Alice's power. Illusions materialized around him—ghastly specters, twisting shadows, and ethereal screams that seemed to pierce through the very fabric of the room. He stood in the center, a lone figure in the shifting landscape of his mind.

"Let the interrogation begin," Alice declared, her voice cutting through the eerie silence.

The first illusion hit Sebastian like a violent storm. He recoiled as spectral stakes materialized from the shadows, driving through his body with relentless force. Each phantom stake was a vivid manifestation of pain, Alice ensuring that every nerve in his being felt the excruciating agony. His stoic facade wavered, and beads of sweat formed on his forehead.

Elijah, standing beside Alice, maintained a stern demeanor. He understood the necessity of extracting information swiftly, without room for mercy. "Where is Moros Noctis?" Elijah demanded, his voice carrying a weight that echoed through the room.

Sebastian, struggling against the onslaught of illusions, spat defiantly, "You'll get nothing from me, Godlike scum."

Maximus, his patience wearing thin, stepped forward. "Alice, intensify the illusions. Make him feel the torment of a thousand stakes."

Alice nodded, her eyes narrowing with determination. The illusions escalated, becoming a surreal symphony of torment. Sebastian, now ensnared in a nightmarish reality crafted by Alice's formidable powers, began to falter. His resistance waned as the pain became too tangible, too overwhelming.

The illusions shifted. This time, Sebastian found himself suspended in mid-air, surrounded by a writhing mass of shadowy tendrils. The darkness constricted around him, squeezing the life out of his body. Alice's voice echoed through the chamber, taunting him, "Tell us, Sebastian. Your pain will end when Moros Noctis is revealed."

Sebastian grunted, his eyes betraying a flicker of vulnerability. The illusions were burrowing into the recesses of his psyche, stripping away the layers of defiance he had carefully crafted.

Elijah, ever the strategist, stepped forward. "Sebastian, the agony you endure is merely a fraction of what awaits you. We have the power to delve deeper into your darkest fears, your most haunting memories. Choose your path wisely."

Despite his resolve, Sebastian's stoicism began to crumble. Memories long buried resurfaced, and the torment intensified. Alice, wielding the illusions like a maestro, manipulated the fabric of Sebastian's nightmares with precision.

As the hours passed, the interrogation became a relentless dance between Alice's illusions and Sebastian's dwindling resistance. Elijah's inquiries became sharper, each question probing deeper into the mystery of Moros Noctis's whereabouts. Yet, Sebastian clung to his silence, the price of betrayal outweighing the torment he endured.

Maximus, growing impatient, seized the opportunity to amplify the pressure. "Enough of this," he declared, his voice cutting through the room. "Alice, we need answers. Push harder."

Alice nodded; determination etched across her features. The illusions intensified once more, the boundaries between reality and nightmare dissolving into a chaotic swirl. The stakes returned, more numerous and more agonizing than before. Sebastian's defiant facade cracked, and his breaths became strained.

In the midst of the unrelenting onslaught, a revelation emerged. A subtle twitch, a fleeting glimpse of vulnerability—the signs were there. Elijah, ever perceptive, seized the moment. "Sebastian, you can end this. Just tell us where Moros Noctis is hiding."

The vampire lord, teetering on the brink of surrender, gritted his fangs in defiance. "I will never betray him."

Maximus, unleashing a surge of frustration, approached Sebastian with a newfound intensity. "Alice, go deeper. Show him the consequences of defiance."

Alice, her eyes ablaze with determination, delved even further into Sebastian's mind. The illusions became a torrent of surreal horrors, mirroring the internal struggle of the vampire lord. His resistance faltered, and the unspoken horrors of his past were laid bare.

Elijah seized the opportunity. "Sebastian, we can make this end. No more illusions, no more pain. Just tell us where to find Moros Noctis."

The room, steeped in the echoes of Sebastian's torment, held its breath. In that critical moment, Sebastian's resolve shattered. His gaze, once defiant, now betrayed a weariness that went beyond the physical. He spoke, his voice a weary rasp, "I don't... I don't know where he is. It was a trap."

The admission hung in the air, a revelation that shifted the dynamics of the room. Elijah's stern expression softened for a brief moment, acknowledging the toll the relentless interrogation had taken on Sebastian.

Maximus, ever pragmatic, approached with a calculated calmness. "What do you mean?"

Sebastian, his defiant spirit momentarily subdued, nodded with a hint of resignation. "Noctis orchestrated this. He wanted you out of the way so he could confront Samuel Creed alone."

The weight of Sebastian's words settled upon us, a realization that we had unwittingly played into Moros Noctis's hands. The trap had been set, and we had fallen into it, leaving Dr. Creed vulnerable.

Alice, sensing the gravity of the situation, released Sebastian from the illusions. The room, once filled with spectral torment, returned to a dimly lit chamber. Sebastian, though battered and broken, maintained a semblance of composure.

Elijah, now contemplative, exchanged a glance with Maximus. The urgency to return to the compound heightened as the revelation sank in. "Sebastian," Elijah said, his voice measured, "if this is a ruse, your fate won't be as merciful. Confirm your words with truth."

Sebastian, breathing heavily, locked eyes with Elijah. "I speak the truth. Noctis wanted you out of the picture. He seeks Creed, and he'll stop at nothing to find him."

The confirmation sent a chill through the room. Our focus shifted from the defeated vampire lord to the imminent threat that loomed over Dr. Samuel Creed. Maximus, his expression resolute, spoke with a sense of urgency. "We need to get back to the compound immediately."

Without waiting for a response, Maximus gestured toward Sebastian, with just a flick, Sebastian's heart was ripped out of his chest. The room, once a stage for the harrowing interrogation, now became a backdrop for our collective realization—a realization that Moros Noctis had set the pieces in motion, and the game had only just begun.

As we filed out of the dimly lit room, leaving Sebastian to contemplate his fate, I couldn't shake the feeling that the true battle lay ahead. The encounter with Sebastian had revealed more than just the identity of our adversary; it had exposed the vulnerabilities within our own ranks.

The journey back to the compound was a silent one, each step echoing the weight of the revelations that had unfolded. The urgency to reach Dr. Creed before Noctis seized the opportunity gnawed at our collective consciousness.

Upon returning to the compound, the atmosphere was tense. The aftermath of Moros Noctis's assault lingered in the air—the destruction, the chaos, the remnants of a once-secure facility now vulnerable to the malevolent forces that sought to unravel our foundation.

Maximus, leading the way, surveyed the wreckage with a discerning gaze. "We need to find Dr. Creed. Noctis won't waste any time."

Elijah, ever composed, added, "He's right. We have to secure the compound, assess the damage, and locate Dr. Creed before Noctis does."

The urgency spurred us into action. As we navigated the decimated halls of the compound, a sense of urgency permeated the air. The once-familiar surroundings now harbored an undercurrent of danger, a reminder that Moros Noctis was not just an external threat but a shadow within our very midst.

The search for Dr. Samuel Creed became a race against time. The compound, now a battleground, echoed with the memories of a conflict that had caught us off guard. Maximus, his eyes scanning the debris-strewn corridors, spoke with determination. "We need to regroup, strategize, and find Dr. Creed before Noctis executes his next move."

The compound, once a symbol of security and technological prowess, now bore the scars of a confrontation that had exposed our vulnerabilities. As we gathered in a makeshift command center, the gravity of the situation hung heavy in the air.

Elijah, his gaze unwavering, addressed the team. "We fell into Noctis's trap. Now, we must rise from the ashes and confront the threat he poses. Dr. Creed's life depends on it."

The room, filled with agents whose resolve had been tested, echoed with a shared determination. Moros Noctis had set the stage, but the finale awaited—an inevitable clash where the lines between predator and prey blurred, and the fate of Dr. Samuel Creed hung in the balance.

DR CREED

My eyes fluttered open, and the world around me slowly came into focus. I found myself lying amidst the rubble, disoriented and weak. Tengoku, the kitsune residing within me, urged me to wake up fully, reminding me that danger still lurked in the aftermath of Moros Noctis's attack.

Pushing myself off the dirt, I felt the weight of Moros's departure. His parting words echoed in my mind—finishing me off wouldn't bring him much pleasure. He left, leaving chaos and destruction in his wake, along with the aftermath of the gravity-inflicted injuries I now carried.

Stumbling away from the wreckage, I realized the extent of my disorientation. Moros's assault had sent me flying, perhaps miles away from the compound. Gasping in disbelief, I trudged back, almost two miles on foot, the compound slowly coming into view.

Returning to the once-secure facility now reduced to ruins, I heard familiar voices. My guard went up. Moros might have departed, but the danger was far from over. Firing up my tails for protection, I collapsed, the voices growing distant.

When I awoke, I found myself on a medical bed, the familiar voices now clearer. I listened as they discussed plans for rebuilding the compound, barely bothered by the fact that it had been reduced to rubble. Elijah instructed Alice to conjure floor plans, Maximus to utilize his omni-kinetic abilities in following Elijah's blueprints as they reconstructed the secret base.

Sitting up, I admired the resilience of my protégés. Grateful that they hadn't witnessed my defeat at Moros's hands, I pondered how a direct confrontation would have wiped them from existence, given their current state of readiness.

The four godlike agents continued their discussions, mapping out the rebuilding process as if the destruction were a mere inconvenience. Elijah's orders were met with efficient responses. Alice's illusions manifested the floor plans, a visual guide for everyone involved. Maximus manipulated the environment with his omni-kinetic abilities, shaping it according to the ethereal blueprints.

Cyrus observed in awe as they seamlessly orchestrated their extraordinary powers. Each member played their part, contributing to the rebirth of the compound. Despite the recent devastation, their focus remained unwavering, a testament to their resilience in the face of supernatural adversity. As the rebuilding plan unfolded, I couldn't help but feel a sense of pride in my handpicked team. They were not just agents; they were formidable beings capable of rising from the ashes, ready to face whatever challenges lay ahead.

As the godlike agents gathered in the newly fortified compound, a palpable sense of transformation hung in the air. Cyrus, now wielding absolute command, stood at the center, a conduit of ancient power. Maximus, the master of omni kinetic abilities, exuded an aura of control over the very fabric of reality. Alice, the mistress of absolute illusions, reveled in the newfound depth of her artistry.

Elijah, with his strategic mind, and I, watched as they recounted the events in Paris. Cyrus, in his measured tone, detailed the brutal interrogation of Sebastian and Maximus's decisive removal of the vampire lord's heart. The room echoed with the gravity of their experiences, a testament to the darkness they faced.

Maximus, unapologetic yet resolute, admitted to the necessity of his actions. His omni kinetic abilities, once again, proved instrumental in a dire situation. The compound, a canvas for his powers, bore witness to the sheer potential he harnessed. The heart of Sebastian, now a macabre trophy, was a stark reminder of the lengths they would go to protect the world from supernatural threats.

As we discussed the mission, Alice's illusions danced around the room, creating ethereal replicas of the Parisian battleground. The gods and mythical beings she conjured took form, showcasing the depth of her absolute illusions. It was a mesmerizing display, and even I, accustomed to the extraordinary, found myself captivated by the vivid tales she spun.

In the aftermath of Sebastian's demise, the compound underwent a metamorphosis. Together, Cyrus, Maximus, Elijah, and Alice worked in harmony, blending their abilities to reshape the very architecture of the base. The result was a stronghold that defied conventional understanding – a marvel of defensive mechanisms, gravitational manipulation, and illusions woven into the fabric of its existence.

Elijah, always pragmatic, ensured that every aspect of the compound served a strategic purpose. His guidance, coupled with Alice's illusions, created deceptive corridors and concealed entrances. The walls seemed to ripple with unseen energy, a testament to the convergence of their extraordinary talents.

Cyrus, with his inugami at his side, patrolled the perimeter, the mystical creatures serving as vigilant sentinels. Their loyalty and ferocity added an otherworldly layer of defense, making the compound not just impenetrable but a symbol of their newfound unity.

Maximus, with his omni kinetic abilities, fine-tuned the very foundation of the base. Towers rose and pathways shifted at his command, the compound becoming a dynamic labyrinth designed to disorient any potential intruders.

As we stood in the heart of this extraordinary creation, I marveled at the convergence of their talents. The compound was not just a fortress; it was a manifestation of their growth, a testament to their collective strength. The godlike agents, bound by a common purpose, had forged something truly extraordinary – a bastion that stood defiant against the supernatural forces that sought to plunge the world into chaos.

As Cyrus, Maximus, and Alice succumbed to the exhaustion of their extraordinary abilities, Elijah and I acted swiftly to prevent them from collapsing onto the ground. In a seamless display of strength, Elijah effortlessly hoisted Cyrus and Maximus onto his shoulders, while I cradled Alice in my arms, carefully carrying them to the medical bay.

Placing them gently onto the beds, Elijah and I shared a concerned glance. It was evident that the exertion of their godlike powers had taken a toll on their physical forms. As I monitored their vital signs, Elijah suggested something that, in my opinion, bordered on recklessness. He proposed channeling his powers to reverse the effects of death within the fortress.

An uneasy discussion unfolded between us, Elijah's determination contrasting with my pragmatic concerns. Channeling such a colossal amount of energy was a risky endeavor, and the potential consequences loomed ominously. I warned Elijah of the dangers, fearing that the attempt might drain him to the point of no return, or worse, leave him as an empty husk.

The air in the room grew tense as our conflicting viewpoints clashed. Elijah argued passionately, emphasizing the potential benefits of restoring life within our fortress. I, in turn, stood firm in my apprehensions, urging caution and strategic planning. Both of us presented valid points, creating a deadlock in our decision-making.

After a heated exchange, Elijah relented, choosing to heed my advice. It was a testament to the trust we held in each other, an acknowledgment that our strengths were most effective when combined. Recognizing the gravity of the situation, Elijah and I joined forces to prepare the team for recovery.

With a shared understanding, we worked in tandem to administer restorative measures. Hydration, nourishment, and monitoring became our immediate priorities. As the medical bay hummed with activity, I couldn't shake the lingering worry for Elijah. The line between bravery and foolishness was a thin one, and in our world of supernatural challenges, the consequences of missteps were often dire.

Now with the immediate crisis managed, our focus shifted to the intricate process of recovery and rejuvenation. Elijah and I worked tirelessly, ensuring that each godlike agent received the care and attention necessary to replenish their strength. The medical bay became a hub of activity, echoing with the soft hum of monitoring equipment and the occasional whispered conversation.

Cyrus, Maximus, and Alice lay in a state of rest, their vital signs gradually stabilizing under the watchful eyes of advanced medical technology. Elijah's commitment to their well-being mirrored the deep bonds that tied our team together. In these moments of vulnerability, the strength of our unity became more apparent than ever.

As we monitored the godlike agents, Elijah and I engaged in discussions about our next steps. The aftermath of the Paris mission left us with more questions than answers, particularly regarding Moros Noctis and his ominous plans. Our fortress, now fortified and upgraded, stood as a testament to our resilience. However, the shadow of impending threats lingered.

Elijah, his resolve undeterred, expressed his desire to delve into the mysteries surrounding Moros Noctis. The urgency of our situation weighed heavily on us; every moment spent in recovery was a moment that Noctis might exploit. Despite my cautionary instincts, I recognized the necessity of understanding our adversary and uncovering the motives behind his malevolent actions.

In the midst of our strategizing, Elijah proposed a plan to enhance our reconnaissance capabilities. Utilizing his unique connection with the supernatural, he suggested tapping into the collective consciousness of the fortress itself. It was a bold move, one that could potentially provide valuable insights into the unseen threads that connected our world.

As Elijah initiated the process, the atmosphere in the fortress shifted. An ethereal energy pulsed through its walls, intertwining with Elijah's focused intent. The air seemed charged with an otherworldly resonance, and for a moment, I felt a connection to something beyond the tangible. Elijah's eyes glowed with a faint luminescence as he delved into the depths of the fortress's mystical fabric.

The information that unfolded was both enlightening and disconcerting. The fortress, now imbued with a heightened awareness, revealed traces of Moros Noctis's lingering presence. It was as if the very essence of darkness had left an indelible mark, a trail that demanded our attention.

The revelations spurred our team into action. With newfound insights, we refined our strategies and reinforced the defenses of the fortress. Each godlike agent, recovered and reinvigorated, embraced their roles with a renewed sense of purpose. Our collaborative efforts transformed the fortress into a bastion of strength, a nexus where the extraordinary met the pragmatic.

As the sun dipped below the horizon, casting long shadows across the newly fortified compound, Elijah and I exchanged a glance. The challenges ahead loomed large, but within the resilient walls of our fortress, a sense of determination prevailed. Moros Noctis might have left his mark, but we were ready to face whatever darkness he unleashed upon us. Together, we stood, united in purpose and fortified by the unbreakable bonds that defined our extraordinary team.

CYRUS FINCH

Waking within the familiar confines of the fortress, my senses gradually acclimated to the bustling energy that surrounded me. Memories of Paris lingered, like fragmented dreams, leaving me with a sense of displacement. The fortress, usually a bastion of stability, now hummed with a different kind of intensity.

As I rose from the bed, the hum of activity became more pronounced. Godlike agents from diverse corners of the world moved with purpose, a myriad of abilities on display as they prepared for the impending battle. The air crackled with a fusion of energies, creating an electrifying ambiance that hinted at the vast potential within our extraordinary team.

Eager to understand the scope of our resources, I wandered through the fortress, witnessing agents engaged in a kaleidoscope of activities. Some manipulated elements with casual ease, while others demonstrated telepathic prowess or showcased physical feats that defied conventional limits. It was a dazzling spectacle of power, each agent a testament to the breadth and depth of human potential.

Amidst the training sessions and introductions, Dr. Creed approached, his presence commanding attention. He explained the urgency of the situation, the need to fortify our defenses and prepare for an impending war. The gravity of his words resonated, and I nodded in acknowledgment, ready to contribute to our collective resilience.

Curiosity burning within me, I questioned Dr. Creed about the absence of the Guardians of Destruction in our efforts. His response, a revelation that Moros Noctis was once known as Peter Wayne, a high-ranking figure within the G.O.D., and Elijah Wayne's father left me stunned. The clandestine nature of our project, the Godlike Project, unfolded as Dr. Creed unveiled the layers of deception surrounding Moros Noctis's existence.

Intrigue and apprehension danced in my mind as Dr. Creed disclosed the covert mission sanctioned by the Guardians of Destruction. The godlike agents, assembled from various backgrounds and disciplines, became a covert force designed to combat a threat too perilous to be addressed publicly. The revelation deepened the shadows encircling Moros Noctis, painting a portrait of a foe enshrouded in secrecy and complexity.

With newfound knowledge and a sense of purpose, I embraced the training sessions that followed. The fortress transformed into a crucible of preparation, a place where abilities were honed, and alliances forged. I sparred with agents who wielded elements I had never encountered, absorbing their techniques and integrating them into my own skill set.

As the day unfolded into night, a collective determination pervaded the fortress. We weren't merely a collection of individuals; we were a formidable force united against a common adversary. The synergy of our abilities, the convergence of diverse talents, promised a formidable front against Moros Noctis.

The Godlike Project, shrouded in secrecy, now stood as a beacon of hope in the face of impending darkness. With each passing moment, we drew closer to the inevitable clash, the convergence of extraordinary forces against an enigmatic foe. The fortress, pulsating with the heartbeat of determination, echoed with the unspoken resolve that resonated within each godlike agent. The stage was set for a battle that would define the destiny of our world.

As Dr. Creed's words resonated through the massive gathering of godlike agents, a tangible gravity settled over the fortress. His commanding presence commanded attention, and as he welcomed us back, I couldn't help but feel the weight of the collective purpose that bound us together.

"Welcome back. It's been so long since I've seen some of you. Now with the overwhelming danger we face, we must remember you we're all built different, all with the purpose of exterminating this particular threat. We will not waver. The enemy took from our ranks, and in response, we will destroy everything he holds dear."

Elijah, standing nearby, shifted uncontrollably, a telltale sign of the unease that resonated within him. Dr. Creed's announcement hung in the air, sparking a sense of anticipation among the gathered agents.

With the veil of suspense draped over the assembly, Dr. Creed unveiled the blueprint for a daring mission, a plan forged through the efforts of Elijah in locating Moros Noctis. The mission required a team of unparalleled strength, and Dr. Creed introduced the concept of the "Body of God." The mere mention of it stirred intrigue and curiosity among the godlike agents.

The selection process for this elite team was revealed with dramatic flair – a tournament of epic proportions. The first round promised chaos, a Battle Royale where the only rule was simple: survive until only forty-eight agents remained standing. The survivors would then advance to a series of four-on-four battles, with the remaining twenty-four agents fighting in intense one vs one matchups.

Elijah, though visibly restless, seemed to understand the gravity of this opportunity. The prospect of being part of the "Body of God" resonated with the agents, and a charged energy filled the air as discussions erupted among the godlike community. The fortress, once a haven of training and preparation, now buzzed with a new sense of urgency and determination.

The following days were a whirlwind of anticipation and preparation. Agents trained with renewed vigor, honing their abilities and strategizing for the upcoming tournament. The atmosphere was electric, as alliances were formed, and rivalries emerged. In the corridors of the fortress, you could hear the hum of conversations, feel the tension, and witness the shared commitment to face the imminent danger head-on.

As the day of the tournament approached, the fortress transformed into an arena of anticipation. In the heart of the Battle Royale, the air pulsated with an electric fervor, and the ground beneath my feet trembled with the force of countless abilities converging. My senses heightened as the agents engaged in a chaotic dance of power, each maneuver a testament to their unique skills.

Elijah, Maximus, and Alice emerged as formidable contenders, their victories echoing through the tumultuous battlefield. Every time one of them triumphed, a surge of exhilaration pulsed through me, a beacon of hope amid the unpredictable chaos.

The skirmish unfolded with breathtaking intensity. Agents fell like dominoes, some eliminated within moments of the battle's inception, revealing the cutthroat nature of our reality. The stakes were high, and survival meant navigating through a maelstrom of abilities and betrayals.

As I maneuvered through the turmoil, my absolute command became a formidable shield. With a mere thought, I redirected attacks, turned alliances in my favor, and maintained a strategic advantage. It was a dance of influence, a delicate ballet amidst the chaos.

The diverse range of powers on display was nothing short of mesmerizing. Elemental manipulations clashed with reality-warping illusions, and kinetic forces collided with supernatural energies. The battlefield was a canvas painted with the vibrant hues of extraordinary abilities.

In the midst of the fray, Elijah showcased his prowess, each movement a testament to his skill in both offense and defense. Maximus, with his omni kinetic abilities, manipulated the very fabric of the battlefield, turning the environment into a weapon at his command. Alice, the mistress of absolute illusions, wove intricate fantasies that confounded and disoriented her adversaries.

Excitement surged within me each time Elijah unleashed a devastating blow, Maximus orchestrated a strategic maneuver, or Alice artfully deceived her opponents. Their victories resonated through the chaos, offering moments of respite and inspiration.

Yet, the reality of the battle was unrelenting. Agents fought tooth and nail, alliances formed and dissolved with the swiftness of a summer storm. The scent of sweat and tension hung thick in the air as the numbers dwindled, and the survivors faced the ever-looming threat of elimination.

As the Battle Royale raged on, the arena became a stage for both desperation and determination. Each agent sought to prove their mettle, driven by the desire to be among the last standing. The clash of powers intensified, creating a symphony of destruction that echoed across the battlefield.

In the midst of this tumultuous dance for survival, I maintained a careful balance, utilizing my absolute command to navigate the shifting tides. My strategy was not just about survival; it was about ensuring that Elijah, Maximus, and Alice continued to shine as beacons of strength.

As the number of contestants dwindled, the atmosphere grew increasingly charged with anticipation. Every victory and defeat reverberated through the battlefield, shaping the narrative of our collective struggle. The Battle Royale had become a crucible, forging alliances, testing loyalties, and pushing each agent to their limits.

In the end, as the dust settled and the echoes of clashes faded, the survivors emerged, battle-weary but victorious. Elijah, Maximus, and Alice stood among them, their resilience a testament to the strength that had propelled them through the crucible of the Battle Royale.

Dr. Creed, observing the outcome with a discerning eye, stepped forward to address the remaining agents. The tournament had revealed a cohort of formidable contenders, and the next phase of the selection process – the four vs four battles – promised even more intense confrontations. The atmosphere in the fortress crackled with anticipation as the chosen teams prepared to face each other in the arena. The journey to assemble the "Body of God" had only just begun, and the true test of strength and unity lay ahead in the battles that awaited.

In the midst of the Battle Royale aftermath, my eyes met with those of Alice, Elijah, and Maximus. Unspoken understanding passed between us, a silent agreement that resonated with the gravity of the challenges ahead. No words were needed; we knew that the next step was to forge a team that embodied sheer devastation, a force that Moros Noctis couldn't easily dismiss.

As we gathered during the brief respite before the commencement of the second round, Elijah took the lead in discussing our strategy. His plans unfolded with meticulous detail, weaving a tapestry of coordinated attacks, leveraging each of our unique abilities to their fullest potential.

"We need to be more than a team; we need to be a force of nature," Elijah began, his eyes holding a steely determination. "Cyrus, your absolute command is our linchpin. Use it to manipulate the battlefield, turn their own strengths against them. Maximus, your omni kinetic abilities give us unparalleled control; shape the environment to our advantage. Alice, your illusions—"

"—will be the key to disorienting and distracting them," Alice finished his sentence with a confident nod. "I can create illusions so vivid that even the most seasoned opponents will question what's real."

Maximus interjected, "I'll use my omni kinetic abilities to enhance our movements and disrupt their coordination. We need to be unpredictable and overwhelming."

Elijah continued outlining the plan, each detail contributing to the symphony of destruction we aimed to unleash. "The four vs four will be our proving ground. We hit hard, fast, and with precision. Each move calculated to expose weaknesses and exploit vulnerabilities. Together, we're a force that Moros Noctis won't see coming."

As we absorbed the strategy, a silent determination settled over us. The air crackled with the anticipation of battle, and the weight of our shared purpose bound us together. Elijah's plan was more than a set of instructions; it was a blueprint for victory, crafted with the intention of dismantling the opposing team piece by piece.

With a final nod of agreement, we dispersed to prepare for the upcoming confrontation. The tournament's second round loomed on the horizon, and the arena would soon bear witness to the clash of godlike abilities. The prospect of facing Moros

Noctis was daunting, but with our united strength and a strategy forged in the crucible of the Battle Royale, we approached the challenge with unyielding resolve.

As the echoes of our footsteps faded, the weight of the impending battle settled upon each of us. We knew that this was not just a fight; it was a defining moment in our mission, a chance to confront the malevolent force that had orchestrated so much chaos.

The stage was set for the four-on-four battle, and as we regrouped before the tournament's second round, a palpable sense of camaraderie infused the air. Together, we would face the darkness that lurked in Moros Noctis, each of us a pillar of strength supporting the others. The countdown to the confrontation had begun, and we stood on the precipice of a battle that would shape the fate of not just our team but the entire godlike community.

DR CREED

The four-on-four battles unfolded with a symphony of chaos, each clash a testament to the godlike abilities wielded by the competing teams. I watched as a silent observer to a starting war.

In the inaugural clash of absolute powers, Team A, composed of the formidable agents Sarah, James, Emily, and Michael, showcased a mesmerizing display of extraordinary abilities. Sarah, wielding the destructive force of fire, conjured flames that danced on the brink of reality, creating an ever-shifting tapestry of heat and light. James, a master of temporal manipulation, wielded time itself with absolute control, creating disruptions that challenged the very flow of the battlefield.

Emily, a powerhouse capable of reshaping matter at will, harnessed her strength to mold the very fabric of the battleground. The ground beneath their feet transformed, taking on molten and shifting forms, creating both cover and hazards. Michael, the emotional amplifier, skillfully harnessed and magnified the determination of his teammates, infusing them with a potent cocktail of resolve, fueled by the fiery energy at Sarah's command.

On the opposing side, Team B, featuring the skilled agents Alex, Olivia, Daniel, and Sophia, countered with their own arsenal of absolute powers. Alex manipulated the forces of gravity, altering the very fabric of the battlefield. Olivia, armed with the power of elemental control over wind, summoned gusts and cyclones to counter the scorching flames unleashed by Sarah. Daniel's telepathic abilities sought to establish a mental stronghold, while Sophia utilized her speed to become a whirlwind on the battlefield.

The clash of powers painted a vivid tableau of chaos and brilliance. Sarah's fiery dance challenged Olivia, who found herself battling both the searing flames and the elemental storms conjured by her opponent. Emily's mastery over matter transformed the ground beneath them, creating advantageous positions for Team A while posing additional challenges for Team B. James manipulated the flow of time to disorient Daniel's telepathic efforts, disrupting Team B's coordination.

In the culmination of a fiercely contested battle, Team A emerged victorious through a strategic fusion of fire, temporal manipulations, and the unwavering determination amplified by Michael. The battlefield bore witness to the convergence of extraordinary powers, setting the stage for the next thrilling encounter in this godlike tournament.

The second match unfolded as a mesmerizing display of absolute powers, pitting Team C, consisting of agents Christopher, Natalie, Benjamin, and Ashley, against the formidable Team D. The arena transformed into a battleground where elemental manipulations, technological warfare, and matter transmutations collided in a dazzling spectacle.

Christopher, the wielder of elemental forces, summoned storms of fire and ice that danced across the battlefield. The clash of flames and frozen tendrils became a visual symphony, challenging David's telekinesis. Clad in telekinetic armor, David erected barriers and launched kinetic bullets from his fingertips, creating a breathtaking display of kinetic prowess in the face of elemental chaos.

Natalie, the technological virtuoso, harnessed absolute precision to craft intricate weapons from the fabric of the environment. Her creations clashed with Jessica's attempts at water manipulation, creating a battlefield where advanced technology and liquid forces collided in a stunning juxtaposition of power.

Benjamin, the transmuter, wielded the ability to reshape matter, altering the very essence of the battlefield. Molten liquids flowed under his control, and solid ground shifted to his strategic advantage. In response, Ryan from Team D, master of sound waves, attempted to disrupt Benjamin's concentration, creating a cacophony of discord amidst the transmutations.

Ashley's gift of absolute teleportation added an unpredictable dimension to the fight. Blinking across the battlefield, she became an elusive phantom, avoiding attacks and repositioning strategically. Lauren, with her absolute invisibility, tried to match Ashley's unpredictable movements, turning the clash into a game of shadows and teleportation.

The arena bore witness to a riveting clash of powers, with Team C ultimately emerging victorious. The elemental mastery of Christopher, technological ingenuity of Natalie, and strategic transmutations of Benjamin created a symphony of godlike abilities that overwhelmed their opponents. The stage was set for the next thrilling chapter, as the agents showcased the depth of their absolute powers in a dazzling display of combat prowess.

The third battle unfolded with an electrifying intensity, a symphony of godlike powers colliding in a dazzling display. The agents of Team E, Ethan, Lily, Mason, and Ava, moved with a coordinated precision that left their opponents in awe. The stage was set for an epic clash, and the battlefield crackled with the anticipation of unparalleled abilities.

Ethan, the embodiment of absolute speed, launched into action like a lightning bolt, leaving trails of afterimages that confounded Team F. His movements were a blur, as he weaved through their defenses with a vicious intensity. Fiona's attempts at manipulating plants were futile as Ethan's rapid assaults disrupted her concentration, rendering her manifestations ineffective. Braxton's animal control proved insufficient against the sheer velocity of Ethan's attacks.

Meanwhile, Lily, with absolute strength, transformed the battlefield into her domain. Her every strike was like a thunderous clap, creating shockwaves that reverberated through the air. Braxton's attempts to command animals faltered as Lily's overwhelming force shattered their defenses. Fiona's plant manifestations withered under the sheer power of Lily's blows, creating a devastating synergy that overwhelmed Team F.

Mason's reaction time became the linchpin of their strategy. His calculated movements allowed him to predict and counter every move from Team F. Debbi's emotion manipulation proved ineffective as Mason's precision nullified any attempts to disrupt his focus. Ian's telepathic abilities were countered by Mason's swift responses, creating a cascade of strategic advantages for Team E.

As the battlefield became a chaotic dance of powers, Ava, the master of absolute fusions, orchestrated a seamless integration of their abilities. Fiona's weakened plant manifestations became part of Ava's strategic fusion, enhancing the team's offensive capabilities. Braxton's animal allies found themselves working in tandem with Team E, turning the tide of the battle against Team F.

In a pivotal moment, Ethan and Lily unleashed an epic combo that left their opponents in awe. Ethan's blinding speed created a diversion, drawing the attention of Team F, while Lily, with unparalleled strength, launched a devastating assault. She propelled Fiona's manipulated plants toward Team F with a force that defied resistance. The once-formidable opponents were caught off guard, unable to counter the synchronized assault.

The battle concluded with Team E standing victorious amidst the remnants of their godlike clash. Ethan's relentless speed, Lily's overwhelming strength, Mason's calculated reactions, and Ava's strategic fusions had proven insurmountable. The audience watched in awe as Team E's coordinated prowess left Team F defeated.

The fourth match unfolded as a brutal spectacle of power, a relentless clash between Team G and Team H that left the battlefield in chaos. The agents, each wielding their absolute abilities, engaged in a fierce contest that showcased the extent of their godlike prowess.

Gavin, with absolute control over energy, became a force to be reckoned with. His manifestations of raw power clashed violently with Henry's manipulation of shadows, casting an eerie and chaotic atmosphere over the battlefield. Gavin's surges of energy collided with Henry's elusive shadows, creating bursts of dazzling light and encroaching darkness that left the audience on the edge of their seats.

Rachel, possessing telepathic abilities, engaged in a mental duel with Sophie, the master of illusions. Their minds became a battleground of conflicting perceptions, as Rachel sought to unravel the illusions Sophie wove. The battlefield transformed into a surreal landscape, with illusions and psychic energies colliding in a mesmerizing display of mental prowess.

Oliver's control over magnetism disrupted Liam's attempts at control, creating a magnetic tug-of-war that influenced the very fabric of the battlefield. Metallic objects danced through the air as the agents struggled for dominance, their powers creating a metallic ballet that added another layer of complexity to the ongoing clash.

Mia, with the power of sound manipulation, engaged in a cacophony of conflicting forces with Emma, the wielder of time manipulation. The air reverberated with the clash of sound waves and temporal distortions, creating pockets of distorted reality and dissonant echoes that reverberated through the battlefield.

The agents of Team G and Team H pushed the limits of their abilities, each maneuver and countermeasure adding to the intensity of the battle. In the end, Team G emerged victorious, their coordinated efforts and strategic use of absolute powers securing their place in the ongoing battle for supremacy. The aftermath of the clash left the battlefield scarred and the audience in awe.

The fifth match unfurled with an electrifying intensity, a symphony of godlike abilities that resonated across the battlefield. Team I, comprised of agents Isaac, Grace, Noah, and Zoey, confronted the formidable Team J, featuring Jake, Mia, Ethan, and Olivia. Each agent bore the weight of absolute powers that promised to redefine the course of the ongoing battle.

Isaac, a maestro of lightning, called forth storms of electrifying power that clashed with Jake's command over nature. Thunder echoed through the arena as lightning danced across the sky, a celestial battle between the primal forces of weather and the controlled chaos of elemental electricity.

Grace, a virtuoso of telekinesis, engaged in a kinetic struggle against Mia, whose manipulation of emotions sought to disrupt the calm precision of telekinetic control. The air crackled with tension as unseen forces collided, creating a dynamic dance of psychic energies that left the battlefield in a constant state of flux.

Noah, a weaver of illusions, conjured mesmerizing spectacles that confounded Ethan's attempts at intangibility. Illusions and reality became intertwined in a kaleidoscope of shifting perceptions, as Noah's mind games challenged the very fabric of Ethan's ability to exist beyond the physical realm.

Zoey, a healer with absolute capabilities, became the linchpin of Team I's strategy. Her abilities mended wounds and bolstered her team's resilience against Olivia's formidable energy constructs. As Olivia crafted powerful manifestations of energy, Zoey's healing touch became a crucial counterbalance, turning the tide of the battle in Team I's favor.

The battlefield became a canvas for their godlike powers, a tapestry woven with lightning, kinetic forces, illusions, and the ebb and flow of healing energies. In a crescendo of strength and strategy, Team I emerged victorious, their coordinated use of lightning storms, telekinetic control, illusionary tactics, and the invaluable healing touch of Zoey securing their place in the annals of the ongoing tournament.

As the echoes of the battle subsided, the arena was left charged with tension and anticipation. The godlike agents, having tested the limits of their absolute powers, stood prepared for the challenges that lay ahead, forging alliances and readying themselves for the unpredictable trials yet to come. The fifth battle had been a spectacle of epic proportions, a testament to the extraordinary capabilities of these agents in their pursuit of supremacy.

The arena crackled with an electric anticipation as Team K, composed of Cyrus, Maximus, Alice, and Elijah, faced their final challenge against the formidable Team L— Kevin, James, Tony, and Brian. The air seemed to shimmer with the promise of godlike confrontations, and the audience held their breath in anticipation of the ultimate clash.

The battle commenced with a surge of energy as Elijah's presence swept across the arena like a tempest. An unexpected twist unfolded when Team L, overwhelmed by Elijah's aura, hesitated, their courage shattered in the face of his formidable might.

Elijah, annoyed by their reluctance, swiftly issued a command to Alice, the master of illusions. The arena transformed as Alice conjured a mesmerizing illusion, a tapestry of confidence that washed over Team L like a tidal wave, dispelling their fear and ushering in the true beginning of the battle.

Cyrus, the wielder of absolute command, surveyed the opposing team, his eyes locking onto Brian, a colossus with strength bordering on reality-altering might. A sly smile played on Cyrus's lips as he muttered, "I like that power." In an instant, the very fabric of reality yielded to Cyrus's command, and strength surged through him, reshaping the landscape of the battlefield.

The confrontation erupted into a symphony of godlike clashes, each agent a living embodiment of their extraordinary abilities. Maximus, the master of omni-kinetic energies, created torrents of power that swept through the arena, manipulating the very essence of kinetic forces. Alice's illusions danced through the chaos, ensnaring the senses of Team L and weaving intricate patterns that blurred the lines between reality and imagination.

Elijah, a force of nature, harnessed his powers with unparalleled finesse, manipulating the very fabric of reality itself. His presence echoed through the battlefield like a primal roar, commanding respect and fear from friend and foe alike. The clash of powers intensified each agent a brushstroke in the painting of an epic battle.

On the opposing side, Kevin's size-altering abilities made him a dynamic force, altering the very scale of the battlefield at will. James's piercing eyesight unraveled illusions and laid bare the secrets of his adversaries. Tony conjured storms of unimaginable fury, manipulating the elements with absolute precision. Brian, a behemoth of strength, threatened to tear the battlefield asunder with each mighty blow.

The arena became a maelstrom of power, an elemental dance that defied the laws of nature. Lightning crackled, storms raged, and the very ground quaked beneath the impact of godlike clashes. Team K and Team L collided like elemental forces, each agent a living embodiment of their extraordinary abilities.

Cyrus, now wielding reality-altering strength, became a juggernaut on the battlefield. His every movement reshaped the very fabric of space, a testament to the limitless potential of absolute command. Maximus's omni-kinetic energies flowed with unparalleled grace, creating a symphony of kinetic forces that swept through the battlefield like a tidal wave.

Alice's illusions, now enhanced by the confidence boost, wove intricate patterns that ensnared the senses of Team L, leaving them disoriented and vulnerable. Elijah's force of nature manipulated the elements with finesse, turning the tide of battle with each calculated move.

In the crescendo of the battle, Team K stood as an indomitable force, their godlike powers converging into a symphony of strength and strategy. The clash concluded with a resounding victory for Cyrus, Maximus, Alice, and Elijah, their extraordinary abilities etching a legacy in the annals of godlike history.

As the dust settled and echoes of the clash lingered in the air, the arena bore witness to the triumph of Team K. The audience erupted in applause, their cheers echoing through the arena as the godlike agents reveled in the glory of their final and decisive victory.

CYRUS FINCH

The echoes of our intense battles lingered in the air as Dr. Creed stepped forward, his voice resonating through the arena. "Congratulations to the victors of the 4v4 battles!" he exclaimed, and a surge of pride filled me as our names echoed through the arena.

Dr. Creed continued, "Your extraordinary abilities have left an indelible mark on this tournament. Tomorrow, the grand finale awaits, where the remaining teams will face each other in a climactic showdown. But for now, let us celebrate your achievements!"

The announcement of a feast elicited cheers from us godlike agents. The anticipation of the final battles mingled with the promise of a night filled with revelry. The arena transformed as a clean-up crew swiftly removed the remnants of the intense clashes, creating a blank canvas for the festivities that lay ahead.

I observed the camaraderie among the agents, a sense of unity forged through the shared experiences of the tournament. The journey had been arduous, the battles fierce, and tomorrow promised the culmination of our godlike abilities. As the agents made their way to the mess hall, I followed suit, a silent observer amid the jubilant crowd.

Entering the mess hall, a breathtaking sight awaited us. A colossal feast, a banquet fit for gods, spread before us. Tables groaned under the weight of a myriad of dishes, each more tantalizing than the last. The air was redolent with the enticing aroma of diverse cuisines. From celestial desserts to otherworldly entrees, the feast seemed to transcend the limits of earthly cuisine.

My teammates—Alice, Elijah, and Maximus—and I settled at a table, our seats offering a prime view of the celebratory spread. We exchanged glances, our eyes reflecting the shared triumphs and challenges of the battles we had endured together.

As we began to indulge in the feast, I felt a peculiar sensation. The food seemed to have an almost immediate effect on me. A surge of energy coursed through my veins, and the weariness from the battles began to dissipate. I couldn't help but comment, "This... this food is incredible. It's like it's healing me."

Alice, her eyes sparkling with amusement, offered an explanation. "That's the work of the cooks here. They have the power to manipulate the effects of food, bending reality when it comes to culinary delights. It's not just a feast; it's a manifestation of their abilities to create a dining experience beyond imagination."

The conversation flowed as freely as the drinks, and laughter echoed through the hall. Dr. Creed, ever the gracious host, joined us at our table, raising a toast to our victories. The atmosphere was charged with a blend of excitement and camaraderie, a moment of respite before the grand finale.

As the night unfolded, I found myself engrossed in conversations that transcended the boundaries of our godlike abilities. Stories of the past battles, personal struggles, and triumphs became threads woven into the fabric of our shared experience. Each agent brought a unique perspective to the table, and I couldn't help but feel a profound connection with this eclectic group of extraordinary individuals.

The feast turned into a festival of celebration, we agents reveling in the camaraderie that had evolved amidst the trials of the tournament. The mess hall transformed into a kaleidoscope of colors, laughter, and the clinking of glasses.

In the midst of the festivities, Dr. Creed, raising his glass, proposed a toast. "To the god-like agents! May your powers shine bright in the final battles, and may the bonds forged here endure beyond the tournament."

We echoed the sentiment, the resonance of our shared determination filling the hall. The night wore on, and we godlike agents continued to immerse ourselves in the celebration, drawing strength and inspiration from the unity we had found.

Amidst the revelry, subtle foreshadowing surfaced in the form of cryptic remarks and exchanged glances. Whispers of unknown challenges and hidden truths added an air of mystery to the festivities. As the feast reached its zenith, I couldn't shake the feeling that the grand finale held more than the promise of a victor; it harbored secrets yet to be unveiled.

As the night embraced us, we God agents reveled in the moment, savoring the bonds we had formed and the extraordinary journey that had brought us to this pivotal juncture. The grand finale loomed on the horizon, a spectacle that would test the limits of our godlike abilities and define our place in the annals of this extraordinary tournament.

Amidst the festivities, a particular camaraderie began to blossom—one that went beyond the battlefield. As I engaged in conversations with my fellow agents, I found myself drawn to Alice's presence. There was a depth to her character that intrigued me, a subtle complexity hidden beneath the surface of her godlike abilities.

Alice, with her mastery of illusions, was more than a wielder of fantastical images. Her mind held a labyrinth of thoughts and emotions, and I felt compelled to explore its depths. We spoke about our pasts, our motivations for joining the tournament, and the challenges we faced along the way. Her anecdotes painted a vivid picture of a life shaped by the interplay of reality and illusion.

In the midst of laughter and shared stories, a quiet understanding developed between us. It was as if the barriers between our minds had softened, allowing a genuine connection to flourish. Alice's insights into the nature of illusions mirrored the complexities of our own existence—each agent, a unique blend of strengths, weaknesses, and hidden facets waiting to be uncovered.

As the night unfolded, I found myself entranced not only by the feast before us but also by the enigmatic allure of Alice's character. We discussed the intricacies of our abilities, delving into the philosophical nuances of commanding realities and manipulating perceptions. Her perspectives added layers to my understanding of the godlike world we inhabited.

The festive ambiance created a backdrop for the forging of connections, and I sensed a growing friendship between Alice and me. It was a friendship that transcended the confines of the tournament, one built on shared experiences, mutual respect, and an unspoken acknowledgment of the challenges we faced as godlike agents.

Our conversations, at times profound and at others lighthearted, allowed glimpses into the person behind the power. Alice's illusions, once perceived as mere manifestations of fantasy, now carried a deeper significance—a testament to the artistry of her mind and the resilience that defined her journey.

As the night wore on, the dynamics of our group continued to evolve. Maximus and Elijah, my steadfast teammates, welcomed the new connection with warmth and camaraderie. It was as if the bonds we forged within the battlefield had extended beyond the clashes, creating a synergy that transcended the limits of our godlike abilities.

Alice and I found ourselves engrossed in a conversation about the essence of control and command—themes that resonated with our abilities. There was a certain vulnerability in her words, a willingness to share not only the strengths but also the challenges that accompanied the gift of manipulating perceptions.

In the midst of the revelry, our laughter and exchanged glances spoke volumes—a silent understanding that surpassed the need for verbal communication. It was a connection that defied the conventions of the tournament, a friendship that held the promise of enduring beyond the grand finale.

As the feast reached its zenith, a sense of anticipation lingered in the air. Tomorrow's battles loomed on the horizon, promising a culmination of our godlike abilities. Yet, amidst the festivities, I couldn't help but feel a quiet gratitude for the friendships forged, especially the growing bond with Alice—a connection that added a layer of richness to the extraordinary tapestry of the tournament.

With the vibrant energy of the feast, Alice's voice cut through the revelry like a soothing melody. "Cyrus," she said with a gentle smile, "do you want to get out of here for a while? Take a break from the festivities?"

Her proposition struck a chord within me, and I nodded in agreement. We excused ourselves from the lively gathering, the echoes of laughter and celebration fading as we ventured into a quieter realm. Alice led the way, and as we moved away from the mess hall, the sounds of the festival softened into a distant hum.

We found ourselves in a secluded area, bathed in the soft glow of moonlight. The atmosphere was tranquil, a stark contrast to the electric energy of the tournament. The moon hung in the sky like a celestial guardian, casting its ethereal light upon us.

Alice turned to me with a thoughtful expression. "Cyrus," she began, "I often find solace in illusions. They're not just a manifestation of imagination; they're a reflection of the untold stories within us." She extended her hand, inviting me to join her in a shared illusion, and without hesitation, I accepted.

In an instant, our surroundings transformed into a breathtaking dreamscape. We stood on an otherworldly platform, suspended in the cosmos, with the moon as our silent witness. The illusion was a masterpiece of Alice's creation, a canvas of stars and celestial hues that stretched into infinity.

As we walked through the illusionary moonlit landscape, Alice's illusions became an extension of our shared experiences. We strolled side by side, our steps synchronizing with the rhythmic pulse of the illusion. The beauty of the celestial panorama mirrored the intricate dance of our connection—a dance that unfolded not just in the godlike battles but in the spaces between.

Under the gentle light of the illusory moon, conversation flowed freely. Alice shared stories of her life before the tournament, weaving tales of resilience and growth. I, in turn, opened up about my own journey, recounting the pivotal moments that led me to embrace the mantle of a godlike agent.

The vulnerability in our words forged an unspoken bond, a connection that transcended the illusions surrounding us. Alice's laughter echoed like a melody in the cosmic expanse, and in that moment, the illusion became a shared sanctuary—a place where our true selves unfolded.

As we continued our stroll, the illusionary moon casting a soft glow upon us, the conversation took a more intimate turn. Alice spoke of her affinity for illusions, how they allowed her to navigate a world that often felt elusive. I listened, captivated by the depth of her insights, realizing that her illusions were not just a display of power but a means of expressing the intricacies of her soul.

In the quiet expanse of our illusion, I found the courage to share a part of myself that I hadn't revealed before. "Alice," I began, "the power of command sometimes feels like a double-edged sword. The responsibility, the weight of decisions—it can be overwhelming. But in the midst of it all, there's a beauty in the connections we forge, don't you think?"

She nodded, her eyes reflecting the illusory moonlight. "Absolutely, Cyrus. The illusions I create are not just about bending reality; they're a way of seeking connection. In this fantastical world, we find solace in the threads that bind us together."

The illusionary landscape became a canvas for confessions, a sanctuary where our vulnerabilities became strengths. Under the illusory moon, our connection deepened, transcending the boundaries of the tournament. It was a moment suspended in time, where the godlike agents faded into the background, and Alice and I existed in the intimate tapestry of our shared illusion.

As we approached the culmination of our illusory journey, I found myself drawn to Alice in a way that surpassed the camaraderie forged on the battlefield. The illusory moon became a silent witness to a confession that lingered on the edge of my lips. With a quiet resolve, I turned to Alice, and in the soft glow of the moon, I spoke words that echoed the sentiments of a connection that went beyond the extraordinary battles we faced.

"Alice," I said, "there's a magic in the illusions you create, and in this shared moment, I've discovered a depth that transcends the illusions themselves. Our connection is a testament to the beauty that exists in the spaces between reality and imagination."

The illusory moon seemed to glow brighter, as if acknowledging the unspoken truth that lingered in the air. Alice's eyes held a warmth that mirrored the celestial light, and in that moment, the illusionary world felt more real than anything I had ever known.

Our journey through the illusory moonlight reached its zenith, and as Alice and I stood on the precipice of returning to the festival, a quiet understanding passed between us. The cosmic expanse around us seemed to hold its breath, as if awaiting the next chapter of our shared story.

"Alice," I said, my voice carrying a blend of uncertainty and determination, "before we return, there's something I need to do."

I reached out and gently took her hands in mine. There was a subtle electricity in the air, a palpable connection that transcended the illusions we had just traversed. Alice turned toward me, her eyes reflecting a mixture of curiosity and anticipation.

In that moment, beneath the illusory moon that bathed us in its soft glow, I leaned in, and our lips met in a tender kiss. It was a moment suspended in time, a fusion of shared vulnerabilities and unspoken truths. The world around us seemed to fade into the background as our connection deepened in the quiet expanse of the illusory landscape.

As our kiss unfolded, Alice's innate abilities subtly responded to the surge of emotions coursing through her. The illusions, once a cosmic panorama, transformed into an intricate tapestry of beauty. Colors danced in harmony, celestial patterns emerged, and the illusory moon above us seemed to burst with radiant light. It was as if Alice's subconscious, attuned to the ebb and flow of emotions, wove an illusion that mirrored the intensity of our connection.

The illusory beauty unfolded like a blossoming flower, each petal a testament to the emotions that defined this shared moment. It was a manifestation of Alice's artistic power, a canvas where our connection painted itself in the strokes of cosmic light.

As we broke the kiss, the illusory world retained its newfound beauty, now intricately entwined with the emotions we had shared. The illusory moonlight cast a warm glow on our faces, and Alice's eyes held a depth that mirrored the beauty of the illusion she had inadvertently crafted.

"Cyrus," she whispered, her voice a gentle echo in the cosmic expanse, "there's a magic in shared moments, in connections that transcend the ordinary. The illusions respond to the emotions they encapsulate, becoming a reflection of the beauty within."

I nodded in agreement, acknowledging the profound truth in her words. The illusory landscape, now an intimate masterpiece, seemed to echo our sentiments. The cosmic patterns above us pulsed with a gentle rhythm, as if encapsulating the essence of this shared chapter in our unfolding story.

With a shared understanding, Alice and I turned to make our way back to the festival. The illusory moonlight lingered, casting a luminous trail as we retraced our steps. The beauty of the illusions remained, a silent testament to the depth of our connection—a connection that had blossomed amidst the godlike battles and found its expression in the quietude of an illusory dreamscape.

As we rejoined the festivities, the echoes of laughter and celebration welcomed us back. The illusory moonlight, now a memory etched in the fabric of our shared experiences, lingered in the air like a benevolent guardian. The festival resumed its vibrant energy, but Alice and I carried with us a quiet understanding—a connection that had transcended illusions and become a tapestry of beauty woven in the cosmic expanse of our shared journey.

DR CREED

Amidst the lively symphony of laughter, conversations, and the rhythmic clinking of glasses, the festival unfolded as a vibrant celebration of godlike abilities showcased in the tournament. The atmosphere crackled with an infectious energy, setting the stage for the imminent finale that hung in the air like an unspoken promise.

My attention flitted across the diverse crowd, a melting pot of emotions and interactions. The sip of wine and the burst of laughter became a harmonic melody, resonating with the undercurrent of competitiveness pulsing among the godlike agents.

Contemplation lingered on the upcoming grand spectacle, a metamorphosis of the winner's godly body. It marked the expanding boundaries of godlike capabilities and intrigued me.

My musings meandered towards the formidable contenders – Ethan with unrivaled speed and Lily wielding strength akin to the gods. Maximus, Alice, and Elijah stood out, their powers transcending initial expectations. The impending clash between God's speed and God's strength added an alluring layer of uncertainty to the grand spectacle.

Elijah, a distinct figure in the crowd, caught my eye. Bearing the legacy of Archangel Uriel's grace, his inclusion in my experiments raised questions. Was it a strategic move to secure an ally against his formidable father, or an attempt to ensure his allegiance before the revelation of my role in his tumultuous upbringing? The weight of regret lingered, acknowledging the profound impact of my decisions on Elijah's life.

The ambitious experiment aimed at unlocking latent powers had inadvertently unleashed a force beyond comprehension – a primordial essence defying conventional understanding. Elijah's intricate bloodline hinted at powers that surpassed the conventional bounds of godhood, adding an element of unpredictability to the tapestry of events.

Thoughts shifted towards Moros Noctis; a formidable entity fueled by the fusion with Peter's body. Rendered practically immortal, Moros Noctis embodied the boundless potential of the unlimited energy wellspring. His presence loomed, a reminder of the unpredictable forces at play in the godlike realm.

Amidst the ebb and flow of conversations and celebratory moments, I found myself drawn into the tapestry of festivities. Engaging in meaningful conversations, exchanging pleasantries, and sharing moments of camaraderie with godlike agents became a welcomed reprieve. The feast unfolded as a mosaic of experiences, each interaction adding depth to the unfolding narrative.

As the night wore on, I allowed myself to be carried away by the currents of celebration. The clash of powers, the mysteries of godhood, and the intricate dance of alliances and rivalries became a tapestry of stories woven into the fabric of this extraordinary world. The festival echoed with the vibrancy of shared experiences, and in those moments, I found solace and connection amidst the godlike tapestry that defined our existence.

In the midst of the revelry, a subtle realization struck me – the absence of Alice and Cyrus. Their names were conspicuously missing from the joyous congregation. It stirred a flicker of curiosity, prompting me to wonder about the nature of their absence. Had they sought a moment of respite from the festivities or were they entwined in a narrative of their own making?

The feast continued, alive with laughter and jubilation, yet the undertone of curiosity lingered. Alice and Cyrus, two enigmatic figures, remained elusive, their whereabouts a puzzle in the midst of the grand celebration. As I navigated the bustling crowd, the thought of their absence added a layer of intrigue to the unfolding narrative.

I found myself immersed in the dance of light and shadows, the symphony of voices, and the vibrant colors of the festival. The night embraced the revelry, and as the godlike agents reveled in the shared experiences, the tale of the feast continued to unfold with an air of mystery, waiting to reveal what the future held.

As I stepped forward, the animated hum of the feast hushed, the eyes of godlike agents turning towards me. My voice, a potent current in the air, cut through the celebratory symphony.

"Esteemed agents," my words held the weight of the upcoming proclamation, commanding their attention. The vibrant tableau of the feast paused, the agents focusing on the imminent narrative.

"Tomorrow marks the initiation of the final phase of our grand tournament. Your godlike abilities will manifest not only in the transformation of your divine bodies but also in a crucial operation," my words hung in the air, the anticipatory gaze of the agents fixed on my every syllable.

"After the creation of the God's body, our forces will embark on a raid of Moros Noctis's location. This is a pivotal step in our quest to draw him out for the ultimate confrontation," the revelation echoed, a calculated move in the intricate game.

The significance of the operation permeated the crowd, tension threading through the atmosphere. My gaze swept across the godlike agents, their faces reflecting a mix of resolve and uncertainty.

"The time has come for the final confrontation, a clash that will determine the fate of our realm. Moros Noctis must be confronted, and your abilities will play a pivotal role in this battle," my proclamation set the stage for the grand narrative.

As I stepped back into the shadows, the feast resumed. An undercurrent of anticipation lingered, alliances forming and dissolving. The agents navigated the remaining moments of celebration with the awareness that their existence was on the cusp of a defining chapter.

The night unfolded, feasting and revelry continuing amidst the whispers of destiny. Each agent, a participant in the grand narrative, carried the weight of their godlike abilities. The next day would herald the transformation of their bodies and the commencement of the operation, marking the beginning of the final confrontation with Moros Noctis.

In the shadows, I observed the unfolding drama with a calculated gaze. The tapestry of events approached a climax that would redefine the very fabric of their existence. The feast, a precursor to the impending spectacle, faded into the annals of the night, leaving the agents to contemplate the gravity of the days that awaited them.

CYRUS FINCH

As the first clash unfolded in the godlike tournament, my attention was drawn to the riveting duel between James and Grace, a master of temporal manipulation pitted against the wielder of telekinetic prowess.

The battle commenced with a clash of extraordinary powers, each agent vying for supremacy. In a display of strategic brilliance, James emerged victorious, his mastery over temporal manipulation proving decisive. James manipulated time itself, foreseeing and countering Grace's telekinetic assaults with strategic shifts through the temporal fabric. He cleverly stalled Grace's movements, creating openings to deliver lethal physical blows, leaving no room for her formidable telekinetic abilities to prevail.

The narrative seamlessly transitioned to the next bout in the tournament, a collision of technological ingenuity versus matter manipulation. Natalie, a technopath virtuoso, faced off against Emily, a sculptor of matter at will. The battlefield transformed into a canvas of chaos as the clash unfolded with moderate difficulty.

Natalie, strategically employing her ability to manipulate technology, disrupted Emily's matter manipulations. The arena became a chaotic fusion of gadgets and ever-shifting forms, with Natalie's ingenious creation of a power dampener resembling the G.O.D.'s. In a quirky yet effective display, she deftly ran and dodged, closing the distance to place a neck brace on Emily, stripping away her powers before beating her into submission.

The tournament pressed on with Gavin, the wielder of absolute energy control, facing off against Zoey, a healer with unparalleled abilities. The battlefield crackled with energy as the clash unfolded with moderate difficulty.

Gavin's calculated strategy involved absorbing and redirecting Zoey's healing energies, turning her own abilities against her. Zoey fought recklessly, running through the battlefield and healing herself instantly from all wounds. Gavin, however, turned the tide by redirecting her healing energy into a radioactive force, crucially crippling her and securing his victory.

The godlike battles continued, with Rachel, a telepath of formidable skill, engaging in a mental duel against Michael, whose empathic abilities amplified emotions. The clash of minds unfolded with moderate difficulty, the arena becoming a canvas for illusions of worlds never seen before.

Rachel's finesse in telepathy allowed her to delve into Michael's emotions, creating illusions that exploited his empathic abilities. The battlefield transformed into a surreal landscape of shifting perceptions, showcasing the true extent of their extraordinary powers. In the end, Rachel emerged as the victor, her telepathic mastery proving to be the decisive factor in this epic confrontation.

The tournament's relentless pace carried on, each battle pushing the boundaries of imagination and showcasing the godlike abilities of the agents involved.

In the fifth match, Mason faced off against Isaac, and the clash of powers was nothing short of mesmerizing. Mason, armed with absolute reaction time, emerged victorious with calculated precision.

As Isaac unleashed lightning strikes, Mason's strategic brilliance came to the forefront. Predicting Isaac's every move, he countered with precise movements that disrupted Isaac's control over lightning. In a dance of speed and strategy, Mason skillfully tricked Isaac into stepping into his own lightning blast, securing his triumph in a display of absolute reaction time.

The intensity of the tournament escalated further with the sixth match between Lily and Mia. This encounter was marked by extreme difficulty, a true test of their godlike abilities.

Lily, wielding god-like reality warping strength, faced off against Mia, whose sound manipulations were known for their potency. Lily's overwhelming strength proved to be the deciding factor as reality itself warped in response to her power. In a breathtaking display, Lily had to use her reality-bending strength to both defend against and overpower Mia, who moved at the speed of sound. The clash of their titanic abilities left the arena in awe of the sheer magnitude of godlike strength.

The following match featured Sarah against Christopher, a showdown of elemental mastery. Sarah, with absolute control over fire, engaged in a moderate difficulty battle against Christopher, who thought he had the upper hand with control over all the elements.

Sarah's strategy unfolded with intricate fire illusions that overwhelmed Christopher's elemental control. Mesmerizing displays of living flame emerged, catching Christopher off guard and proving that Sarah's command over absolute fire was unparalleled. The clash of elements showcased the versatility of godlike powers, leaving the arena ablaze with the brilliance of their confrontations.

As the tournament progressed, the eighth match unfolded, featuring Alice against Noah in a battle of illusions.

Alice, wielding absolute illusion, faced off against Noah, a master of illusionary tactics. The battle reached new heights as Alice's powers transcended the ordinary. Standing still in the midst of the clash, Noah attempted to use his illusions on Alice, unaware of the magnitude of her abilities. Alice, with her reality-bending illusions, created illusions within illusions, outwitting Noah and leaving him in a state of profound confusion.

This battle transcended the physical realm, with Alice's illusions affecting everyone on a multiverse scale. World upon world upon world manifested, crushing Noah's psyche with an onslaught of knowledge. The arena became a canvas for the surreal as Alice's godlike powers bent reality itself, marking this confrontation as the pinnacle of the tournament's epic battles so far.

The ninth battle ignited as Oliver hurled metal projectiles left from Natalie's and Ellie's previous clash at Elijah. A concealed barrier enveloped Elijah, effortlessly repelling the onslaught.

My gaze locked onto Oliver, deftly assembling pieces behind him to repair the power dampeners, all while maintaining his relentless assault on Elijah. Tension buzzed in the air as Elijah, displaying patience and resilience, strode through the metallic tornado conjured by Oliver.

As the confrontation escalated, Elijah's primal instincts emerged. He launched into a physical onslaught, delivering powerful blows that echoed through the arena, knocking Oliver around and asserting physical dominance. However, Oliver, undeterred, devised a cunning move – slapping the power dampener onto Elijah's neck, catching him off guard.

Kicked away and battered, Oliver seized the offensive. Molding the metal in the arena, he crafted a formidable mech construct, encasing himself in a metallic armor adorned with weapons. Metal gauntlets struck, missiles soared, and Oliver ruthlessly beat Elijah into the ground, leaving nothing but a gruesome aftermath.

The stage fell into an eerie quiet. Surprised gasps swept through the spectators as the realization dawned that Elijah, seemingly, had met his end. Contemplating retribution, I pondered employing my inugami to avenge Elijah's demise at Oliver's hands.

Suddenly, golden dust materialized, followed by an explosive surge of power. Elijah reformed, a new body emerging from the remnants of the brutal assault. Anger etched on his face, Elijah summoned ethereal beings of thin air, disrupting Oliver's magnetism powers. The demonic alien entities tore into Oliver, climbing and overwhelming the metallic mech.

Elijah, visibly angered by Oliver's actions, observed as the otherworldly beings savaged him. Finally, with a wave of his hand, Elijah uttered the word "begone." A portal opened, engulfing Oliver, his mech, and the demonic aliens simultaneously. The arena fell into a hushed awe.

Amidst the electrifying aftermath of Elijah's resurrection, the arena trembled with anticipation for the showdown between Benjamin, the master of transmutation, and me, wielding the unparalleled might of absolute command. Empowered by absolute command, I infused myself with enhanced speed, strength, and godlike reflexes, transcending the limitations of mortal form.

In a seamless display of mastery, I navigated the battlefield with an otherworldly grace, effortlessly evading every alteration of the ground, gracefully climbing over undulating waves, and soaring over transmutation attacks with an unparalleled agility that left onlookers in awe. The very essence of my being responded to my authoritative will, bending the laws of reality to my advantage and painting a breathtaking spectacle of unmatched prowess on the canvas of the godlike tournament.

The atmosphere crackled with energy as the battle ignited, each move a dynamic display of power and strategy. Benjamin, a virtuoso of transmutation, unleashed a torrent of elemental chaos, attempting to reshape the very fabric of reality. Yet, armed with the authority to command the physical, mental, and ethereal realms, I dove fearlessly into the heart of the maelstrom.

The battlefield became a canvas for the clash of titanic forces. Benjamin's transmutative waves clashed with my commanding gestures, creating a spectacle that left spectators on the edge of their seats. Elements twisted and danced in a mesmerizing display of power, each command a strategic counter to the other.

In the midst of the escalating battle, Benjamin's transmutation took a dark turn as he reshaped the very air into a formidable weapon aimed squarely at me. Panic briefly seized hold of my senses as the elements themselves seemed to rebel against my presence. The torrent of transmuted air threatened to overwhelm, forcing me to grapple with an unexpected onslaught that shook the foundation of my composure.

In the midst of the battlefield's chaos, uncertainty gripped me as the air crackled with the potential for conflict. Every molecule became a strategic consideration, a canvas for the impending clash that tested my absolute command.

Yet, from the brink of turmoil, a surge of resilience and tactical clarity emerged. Drawing upon the very essence of my authority, I delved into the manipulation of universal elements and supernatural forces. The panic that briefly seized me transformed into a razor-sharp determination.

In a pivotal moment, I harnessed my control over the atmosphere. With a command, I altered the oxygen percentage, lowering it to a critical level, and unleashed a surge of carbon monoxide, turning the once-breathable air into a toxic weapon. Benjamin, once formidable, now faced the silent threat of a poisoned environment.

The battleground pulsed with the consequences of my authority, and the elements that rebelled against me now danced to my tune. Benjamin's transmutation, a weapon turned against him, became a testament to my strategic prowess. The arena throbbed with the raw energy of our clash, the calculated manipulation of the battlefield intensifying the stakes.

Executing a masterstroke, I left Benjamin gasping in the poisoned air, powerless against the overwhelming forces at my command. The spectators, caught in the spectacle, erupted into a chorus of awe. The exhilaration of witnessing the tactical precision in the manipulation of reality echoed through the battlefield.

As the saga of the tournament unfolded, the remaining clashes promised even more intricate displays of power and strategy. Amidst the echoes of Benjamin's defeat, I stood ready—a godlike force, wielding the elements as weapons, and destiny in the grip of my command.

DR CREED

Standing at the helm of the observation platform, I couldn't help but be impressed by the riveting displays of power in the recent battles of the godlike tournament. Cyrus's training had elevated him to a level where he could potentially deliver a crucial blow in the looming war against Moros Noctis. Elijah's death, though surprising, paled in comparison to the unsettling possibility that he might not return. It was a disquieting thought that lingered in the recesses of my mind.

Oliver's demise, on the other hand, was met with a pragmatic dismissal. He, like all participants, was well aware of the risks when entering the arena. Each godlike confrontation was a gamble with life, a choice willingly made by those seeking the apex of power.

Thunderous applause echoes through the arena of war as I stand witness to the unfolding spectacle. The aftermath of recent clashes paints a vivid canvas of triumph and sacrifice.

The atmosphere shifts as Maximus and Ava step into the arena, the ground quivering beneath their anticipation. Ava, a master of weapon fusion, creates a colossal spear from the remnants of past battles. Metal from Oliver's clash, technical remnants from Natalie's dance, and elemental fragments from Cyrus's symphony coalesce into her weapon.

The battlefield transforms into a theater of lightning-fast maneuvers as Ava's onslaught commences. Her movements are a breathtaking dance of blades, a tempest of strikes that defy the expectations even of the seasoned Maximus. It's as if the air itself is being sliced by the precision of Ava's attacks.

Maximus, the epitome of composed prowess, effortlessly sidesteps each strike with a grace that transcends the chaos. His evasion is a dance on the razor's edge, a ballet of danger where every step is a calculated defiance of impending peril. His hands remain casually behind his back, a nonchalant display that not only taunts Ava but elevates the intensity of the spectacle.

The clash between Ava's ferocity and Maximus's finesse reaches a crescendo, a symphony of combat echoing through the battlefield. The anticipation is palpable as Ava, fueled by frustration, seeks to escalate the confrontation.

In a revelation that electrifies the battlefield, Ava's eyes blaze with determination. She deciphers the intricate dance of combat, a game unfolding in the chaos of war. With a surge of power that sends ripples through the very fabric of reality, Ava channels the essence of her surroundings—an alchemy of technology, elementals, and the lingering remnants of godlike beings.

The atmosphere crackles with potent energy as Ava transmutes the chaotic amalgamation into a Gallic gun—a manifestation of the battlefield's very essence. In her hands, the gun materializes, a convergence of destruction and creation, reshaping the nature of the relentless conflict that unfolds on these hallowed grounds.

At the zenith of her strength, Ava stands armed with a weapon defying convention—a living embodiment of the battleground's essence. The Gallic gun pulses with latent power, charged with the unfortunate entities unwittingly caught in her radius. Ava, an avatar of war, readies herself to unleash the full force of this newfound might.

With an unwavering gaze, she takes aim and fires the Gallic gun—a thunderous blast tearing through the air, unleashing mangled body parts infused with diverse abilities, covered in metal and elementally charged. The projectile hurtles toward Maximus with lethal intent. Yet, with seamless elegance and defiance, Maximus effortlessly dodges, his hand still nonchalantly behind his back. The dance of combat continues, the battlefield transformed into a canvas where the clash of extraordinary powers unfolds with each calculated move.

In response to the hail of bullets, Maximus conjures a kinetic storm—an intricate tempest of energy converging from all directions. The clash intensifies, an awe-inspiring dance of power and agility. Spears of energy pierce the air as Maximus deftly avoids Ava's furious assault.

Undeterred, Ava channels the frustration simmering within her, turning it into a tempest of turbulent emotions. The battlefield bears witness to her transformative rage as she fuses everything within her reach. In a spectacular display, Ava transcends the boundaries of her mortal form, evolving into an inhuman chimera. The air crackles with newfound energy, and the ground quivers under the weight of her augmented existence.

Maximus, unfazed by the monstrous transformation, continues to be a conduit for a torrential release of Omni kinetic energy. Reality warps at his command as he orchestrates a destructive masterpiece—slicing through the air with ethereal blades, pounding the ground with seismic force, burning with the intensity of a cosmic inferno, and electrocuting the monstrous chimera with bolts of raw energy.

The battleground remains a canvas upon which Maximus paints with the elements themselves—a display of power transcending the mortal realm. Ava, caught in the maelstrom of this reality-bending onslaught, refuses to succumb. With newfound determination, she counters the onslaught, deflecting ethereal blades and weathering the cosmic inferno.

The crescendo of the battle, a crescendo of destruction and rebirth, reaches its zenith. Ava, displaying resilience and defiance, fights back against the encroaching storm. The arena falls into abrupt silence, the echoes of the epic clash lingering in the air like a haunting melody. Both warriors stand, battered and determined, the embodiment of unyielding strength amid the chaos.

As Ava and Maximus stand, locked in a battle that defies the very fabric of reality, Ava unleashes a devastating attack with the Gallic gun fused to her monstrous form. The air trembles as the Gallican onslaught takes form—a cataclysmic surge of destructive energy aimed at Maximus.

In a calculated move, Maximus, the embodiment of unwavering resolve, opens a black hole, a swirling void that hungers for the unleashed power. The torrential force of Ava's attack is irresistibly drawn into the abyss, creating a cosmic spectacle that echoes through the battlefield.

As the black hole dissipates, Ava, now vulnerable, finds herself facing Maximus, who has become the conductor of this otherworldly symphony. With hands raised, Maximus conjures a spear projectile, a manifestation of different elements merged into a deadly amalgamation. The spear, a fusion of fire, ice, lightning, and the very essence of the battlefield, takes shape with an ethereal glow.

With a thunderous thrust, Maximus hurls the elemental spear toward Ava. The projectile pierces through the air with unparalleled precision, a lethal force aimed at the heart of her monstrous form. Ava, despite her resilience, is unable to evade the elemental onslaught.

The spear strikes true, sending shockwaves through Ava's colossal figure. The battlefield quakes as the elements converge upon her, and with a resounding impact, she crumples, the monstrous form dissipating into the dissipating echoes of the epic clash.

The arena falls into a profound silence, the aftermath of the cosmic confrontation leaving an indelible mark on the battleground. Maximus stands as the victor, the embodiment of calm amidst the remnants of the tempest he faced. The hands that orchestrated the chaos now lower, a symbol of mastery over the forces that sought to challenge his command.

As the echoes of the battle linger, Maximus surveys the transformed landscape, a testament to the extraordinary clash that unfolded. The air crackles with the remnants of raw energy, and Maximus, having faced the formidable Ava, remains a solitary figure in the aftermath—an unyielding force in the wake of the cosmic storm.

The aftermath of Maximus and Ava's clash lingers in the air, setting the stage for the next awe-inspiring spectacle - Ethan versus Ashley.

As Ashley enters the battlefield, Maximus gives her an unexpected hug, a moment of camaraderie before the impending confrontation with Ethan. I watch, intrigued, as two formidable opponents prepare to dance in the symphony of war.

Ethan, a living blur of godlike speed, stands poised, barely perceptible, aided by Tengoku's mystical kitsunes within me. Across from him, Ashley, armed with absolute teleportation, readies for a battle that promises to surpass all before it.

The air crackles with anticipation as the clash begins. Ethan exploits his speed, creating illusions that confound Ashley's teleportation. In response, Ashley unleashes chaos—teleporting buildings, planes, and whole explosions onto the battlefield, a relentless assault aimed at overwhelming Ethan.

Ethan defies comprehension with his godlike speed, traversing the chaos in a blink, a shadow eluding Ashley's orchestrated mayhem. The battleground transforms into a dance of teleportation and evasion, where reality and illusion meld into a mesmerizing spectacle.

I recall the warnings about surpassing the speed of light as I watch Ethan challenge the very laws of the universe. The clash becomes a battle that defies fundamental rules, a testament to the extraordinary abilities of these two beings.

The field turns into a chaotic canvas, civilians and animals caught in the crossfire. Ashley, strategic and cunning, sets a devious trap, cornering Ethan in a portal loop. It seems the end is near, but Ethan transcends time itself, leaving Ashley frozen in a standstill.

Ethan's time clones unleash a brutal assault, the universe straining under the unimaginable speed. In a relentless ballet of brutality, he seizes control of Ashley's portals, propelling her through the fabric of space and time. The battlefield transforms into a hellish stage of torment, filled with the sickening sounds of impact and haunting echoes of her struggles.

Yet, Ashley fights back. With each portal, she twists the battlefield into a surreal nightmare. Explosions erupt in ethereal hues, and buildings shift and morph in defiance of reality.

The battlefield roars with the symphony of combat, a cacophony of power colliding. Unfazed, Ashley, the master of portals, orchestrates a dazzling display. She manipulates landscapes, turning the battleground into a shifting maze that challenges even Ethan's godlike reflexes. Buildings morph into projectiles, hurtling towards him, and explosions cascade in waves of calculated chaos.

In a climactic twist, Ethan seizes the moment with calculated brutality. He propels Ashley through her own portals, a ruthless ballet of violence as she hurtles through dimensions. At each emergence on the other side, Ethan is lightning-quick, catching her, only to drag her face-first back into the arena, and then unleashing her once more through another portal.

The relentless dance of torment unfolds the battlefield itself bearing witness to Ashley's demise. The air crackles with the aftermath of their cosmic clash, the echoes of struggles and explosive chaos reverberating. Reality strains under the weight of their powers, leaving nothing but the lingering traces of an epic struggle etched into the very fabric of the universe.

In the haunting aftermath of Ethan's relentless onslaught, the ebb of time reluctantly resumes, unveiling a profound revelation as the universe fractures open. As a humble observer, I stand on the precipice, gazing into the cataclysmic aftermath of a battle that has torn through the very essence of existence. The symphony of speed crescendos to its zenith, imprinting scars upon the battlefield and etching irreversible changes into the fabric of the universe under the colossal weight of Ethan's godlike might.

Through the ruptured veil of reality, a surreal panorama emerges, revealing a different world beyond the tear. In this alternate realm, the diligent strokes of a writer's hands dance with a smart pen, inscribing unknown narratives onto the tapestry of this otherworldly existence. The juxtaposition of battle-scarred chaos and the serene act of creation paints a paradoxical scene beyond the torn boundaries of the universe.

In response to this cosmic revelation, I find myself propelled into action. The tear in the universe becomes a gateway to the unknown, and with an urgent resolve, I leap into the breach, ready to confront the enigmatic forces that beckon from the world beyond the tear.

CYRUS FINCH

In the eerie silence following Dr. Creed's perilous leap into the breach, a suffocating horror takes hold of my senses. A guttural scream tears through the void as I watch him violently hurled back, an unseen force propelling him with malevolent intent. The breach, once a mere conduit to an alternate realm, transforms into a monstrous maw, hungry for the unraveling of reality itself.

An oppressive darkness descends, swallowing the battlefield in shadows that writhe and twist. The air thickens with an unnatural chill, and the pulsating energy emanating from the breach sends shivers down my spine. This isn't just a breach; it's a tear in the very fabric of existence, and the world around us quivers under its malefic influence.

The pulse-like attacks from the breach take on a nightmarish cadence, each wave a harbinger of impending doom. The very ground beneath my feet trembles as if the earth itself recoils from the grotesque spectacle unfolding. I feel the vibrations deep within my bones, an unsettling reminder of the impending cataclysm.

As the onslaught intensifies, reality fractures like a fragile mirror, reflecting distorted visions of horror. Ghastly apparitions flicker in and out of existence, distorted echoes of forgotten nightmares. The breach becomes a gateway to a realm where darkness reigns supreme, and the malevolent forces lurking within hunger for the demise of our world.

The sky above twists into grotesque contortions, a sinister dance of cosmic forces tearing at the very fabric of the heavens. The stars, once steady beacons of light, now flicker like dying embers, swallowed by the encroaching abyss. The very air pulsates with an otherworldly energy, carrying whispers of despair that echo through the desolate battlefield.

Unholy shadows rise from the ground, writhing in grotesque forms as if spawned from the nightmares of the damned. They slither towards the breach, drawn by its malefic allure, as if eager to plunge into the chaotic abyss. The once-familiar landscape warps into a twisted caricature of reality, a grotesque tableau that heralds the end of all things.

Desperation claws at my chest as I watch the world unravel, gripped by a terror beyond comprehension. Dr. Creed, now a broken and battered shell, lies motionless on the tainted soil. His sacrifice, instead of sealing the breach, has unleashed a pandemonium that defies the laws of sanity.

In the face of this eldritch horror, I can feel the boundaries between life and death blur. The breach hungers for souls, and the spectral whispers that permeate the air beckon us towards an abyssal fate. Each pulse from the breach is a heartbeat of impending oblivion, resonating through the air like a grim symphony of the apocalypse.

The ground quakes beneath me as I stand on the precipice of annihilation. The breach, now a swirling vortex of malevolence, devours everything in its path. Reality contorts, warps, and disintegrates, revealing glimpses of eldritch horrors lurking beyond the veil. I find myself teetering on the edge of sanity, a mere pawn in the cosmic horror that unfolds before me.

As I gaze into the heart of the breach, I see faces of the damned, twisted and contorted in eternal agony. Their silent screams reverberate through the void, a haunting chorus that drowns out the last vestiges of hope. The breach hungers for more, insatiable in its appetite for destruction, and I can feel its malevolence seep into the very core of my being.

In this macabre theater of the apocalypse, I am but a witness to the unraveling of reality. The breach, now a monstrous entity, pulses with an insidious energy that corrupts everything it touches. The world around me crumbles into a nightmarish landscape, and I am left to ponder the grotesque fate that awaits us all.

As the breach expands, devouring the remnants of our world, I am swallowed by an inescapable dread. The end of days is upon us, ushered in by the eldritch horror of the breach. In the suffocating darkness, I brace myself for the inevitable descent into the abyss, where all that remains is the haunting echo of our world's demise.

The battlefield erupts into a frenzied ballet of godlike agents, each adorned with unique powers, their very beings a testament to the extraordinary forces at play. Among them, Maximus emerges as a stalwart leader, a commanding figure orchestrating the defense. With a swift and decisive motion, he conjures towering walls of earth, forming an impromptu fortress to shield his comrades from the relentless onslaught of the breach.

Despite Maximus's formidable efforts, some agents find themselves ensnared in the breach's unforgiving grasp, their powers rendered impotent in the face of its ferocity. Lilly, a seemingly innocent schoolgirl with pig tails, channels her godlike strength in a desperate attempt to manipulate the breach. However, her valiant effort is met with a devastating pulse that sends her hurtling backward, a poignant illustration of the breach's unyielding power.

Elijah, shrouded in mystery and wielding abilities beyond comprehension, steps forward with the intent to stitch the breach closed. His divine powers manifest in intricate patterns as he endeavors to mend the very fabric of reality. Yet even the enigmatic capabilities at his disposal prove insufficient against the relentless force emanating from the tear.

In the midst of this chaotic symphony of powers and counterforces, Alice emerges with urgency etched across her face. A beacon amidst the turmoil, she implores me to close the breach. Overwhelmed and drained from the preceding events, I reluctantly express my incapacity to command such a cosmic closure without succumbing to sacrifice. In a moment of gravity, Alice reveals the solution – the inugami, the very essence that once exacted a sacrifice to save her life.

The tear, meanwhile, continues its destructive rampage, an unchecked force of devastation. Ashley, witnessing the escalating chaos, pleads for my intervention, her urgency echoing through the tumultuous battlefield like a desperate plea for salvation.

In a moment of determination, Alice releases an illusion onto me, while the godlike agents fall victim to the tear's ruthless assault. I feel a surge of newfound resolve as Alice, in the midst of the carnage, emphasizes the principle of saving the many, even if it demands sacrificing the few.

Facing the breach with an unwavering resolve, I feel an icy determination coursing through my veins. My connection with the inugami surges as I command the breach to seal shut. A palpable chill envelops me, and for a fleeting moment, my consciousness delves into the realm of my late beloved, Chase.

In this surreal experience, I materialize in the tranquil confines of the medical bay. The hushed atmosphere and slumbering contestants, remnants of a once-peaceful scene, belie the impending upheaval. As I direct the closure of the breach, a sinister transformation unfolds.

The tranquil serenity shatters into a nightmarish tableau. The once-sleeping contestants, undisturbed in their slumber, are unwittingly thrust into a grisly sacrifice. Stomachs rupture, unleashing a ghastly torrent of blood and entrails that paints the once-serene landscape in macabre hues. This visceral manifestation leaves an indelible mark etched upon my consciousness.

My eyes snap open, locking onto Alice's gaze, a fleeting concern etched across her face. The tumultuous chaos of the breach has subsided, sealed by some unseen force. Godlike agents converge, tending to Dr. Creed's wounds, and an eerie quiet blanket the battlefield.

In the hushed aftermath, Alice breaks the silence with a question laden with both curiosity and unease, "What have you done?"

Enveloped by the profound gravity of the sacrifice, a palpable weight descends upon the battlefield. Doubts insinuate themselves insidiously into my mind, their potency magnified by the unanticipated survival of Elijah, Alice, and Maximus. The inugami, designed to exact its toll on those intimately connected to me, curiously spared them. Pervasive questions linger—why were they spared? Is their concern genuine? This pervasive uncertainty eclipses the triumph of sealing the breach, compelling me to confront the unsettling aftermath of a decision that scrutinizes the foundation of my bonds with those closest to my heart. Amidst these disquieting reflections, a persistent doubt nags at the genuineness of our profound friendships.

DR CREED

Amidst the labyrinth of my own subconscious, the dream world unfurls its chaotic tapestry. Shadows morph and twist, blurring the once-defined boundaries between reality and the surreal. As I traverse this landscape of shifting illusions, the very fabric of sanity unravels in the ethereal embrace of dreams. The dream world, a sanctuary entwined with the tendrils of my own creation, metamorphoses into a paradoxical prison where the borders of perception dissolve.

Confusion veils me in a shroud as I navigate this kaleidoscopic nightmare. Faces flicker in and out of existence, their whispered secrets eluding my understanding. My own thoughts echo in disjointed fragments, forming a dissonant symphony that reverberates through the twisted corridors of my subconscious, amplifying the enigmatic nature of the dream world.

In this phantasmagoric maze, Nyarlathotep emerges as a manifestation of cosmic malevolence. An enigmatic figure, he casts an aura that resonates with the unsettling energy of the cosmos. Our gaze entwines in a dance of existential uncertainty, becoming the prelude to a profound philosophical debate that echoes through the twisting corridors of my subconscious.

Within the heart of this surreal dreamscape, the discourse unfolds into a kaleidoscope of inspiration and doubt. Nyarlathotep challenges the very essence of life's morality, questioning the value of the pain I've inflicted in my pursuit to thwart the fallen guardian. This cosmic entity, beyond the grasp of mortal comprehension, becomes the arbiter of existential pondering.

The conversation becomes a symphony of conflicting ideas, a dance that transcends the boundaries of the dream world. We grapple with the fundamental nature of existence, the weight of our choices, and the inexorable consequences that accompany them. It's a surreal interplay of cosmic perspectives, a clash of ideals that reverberates through the very fabric of the dream world.

As the philosophical discourse with Nyarlathotep resonates within the dream world, distant echoes of voices weave through the surreal landscape. Alice, Elijah, and Maximus, their words like ethereal whispers, ripple through the fabric of my dreamscape. Their discussion unveils the unnerving truth — I am ensnared in a nightmare prison, a labyrinth crafted from the convoluted recesses of my own mind. The revelation adds an ominous layer to the complexity of this otherworldly realm.

The zenith of our philosophical debate with Nyarlathotep heralds an impasse, a cosmic deadlock that precipitates a clash of formidable forces within the dream world. His overwhelming power manifests in nightmarish tentacles of cosmic energy, lashing out with ferocious intent. Swift and desperate, I maneuver through the onslaught, yet a haunting question lingers — can I, within the confines of my own mind, stand against an outer god?

In the tumult of this metaphysical struggle, Tengoku's reassuring presence within me becomes my anchor. With unwavering confidence, Tengoku assures that we will persevere. The battleground transforms into a chaotic dance of cosmic energies and nightmarish tentacles. Nyarlathotep's formidable force threatens to engulf my dreamscape, and amidst the cosmic tempest, I seek a path to break free from the shackles of this metaphysical entanglement.

Within the vast tapestry of my dreamscape, the relentless battle unfolds, and I seamlessly channel the formidable powers of Tengoku. Becoming a conduit for the primal forces that reside within this ethereal realm, I stand alongside Alice, a luminary of illusionary mastery, defying the very constraints of the dream world. Together, we confront Nyarlathotep, wielding an unprecedented synergy of cosmic powers.

Alice, the virtuoso of illusions, unfurls her prowess, proclaiming that even within the dream's confines, her abilities remain unyielding. Faced with Nyarlathotep's relentless assault—each nightmarish tentacle an extension of his boundless power—we devise a plan. Two illusionists, united against the cosmic horror intent on unraveling the very fabric of my mind.

Summoning ethereal daggers, I ascend the tentacles, engaging in a mesmerizing dance of slicing and dicing. Each movement is a calculated strike, grabbing the space god's attention while avoiding the retaliatory onslaught of tentacle strikes. Nyarlathotep's attacks, unleashed with a cosmic fury, are deftly dodged in a breathtaking display of agility within the dreamscape's boundless expanse.

With strategic precision, I hurl my ethereal daggers at the space god, executing a fluid retreat to avoid the subsequent counterattack. In this chaotic ballet, Alice weaves intricate illusions, diverting Nyarlathotep's focus and allowing me to continue my engagement with renewed intensity.

As the tentacles lash out with relentless fury, Alice interjects with a mischievous grin, "You see, I'm just a delightful illusion in your mind, Dr. Creed. An illusion with a penchant for mischief and mayhem."

Undeterred, I press on, each dagger strikes a whirlwind of cosmic energy as I ascend the nightmarish appendages. The dream world itself seems to react to our cosmic dance, warping and shifting in tandem with our every movement.

In a moment of transcendent synchronicity, Alice and I execute our plan with unwavering determination. Conjuring illusions within illusions, we create a realm of infinite knowledge and understanding. The dream world shivers as Alice's absolute illusions entwine seamlessly with the powers of Tengoku, giving birth to a prison of enlightenment—an expanse we dub the "Eternal Omniscient Enigma."

Nyarlathotep, ensnared within this cosmic confluence of knowledge, becomes the captive audience of an endless cascade of wisdom in every language, simultaneously replayed for eternity. The dreamscape itself quakes under the weight of our combined powers, and the nightmarish entity is imprisoned within the boundless expanse of understanding. The shockwaves reverberate through the ethereal landscape, and the nightmare that gripped my mind begins to unravel in a spectacular display of illusionary mastery and cosmic combat.

Reality reasserts itself, and I awaken on the solid ground, surrounded by the concerned faces of Alice, Elijah, and Maximus. The ephemeral dream world dissipates like morning mist, and the battlefield shifts from the surreal dreamscape to the harsh embrace of cold reality. Alice's expression reveals concern as she poses the haunting question, "Where is Cyrus?"

As I grapple with the aftermath of the cosmic battle that unfolded within the recesses of my mind, doubt and uncertainty linger in the air. The philosophical echoes of the dream world resonate in my waking thoughts, and the once-clear lines between illusion and reality blur into a disconcerting amalgamation. Though Nyarlathotep may be contained, the repercussions of our metaphysical clash echo through the corridors of my consciousness, leaving an indelible mark on the fabric of my reality.

Cyrus Finch

Leaving the agency was a somber choice, one that still echoed the haunting costs paid to save my fellow agents. Doubts lingered like specters—were they true friends, or mere allies forged in the crucible of necessity? Some agents chose to follow me into the unknown, heralding me as a divine being for the salvation I had brought upon them. The growing sense of a cult forming around me felt palpable, but I chose not to dispute it.

Journeying with my newfound followers, including Lily, Mason, Natalie, and grateful victors of the tournament, we scoured the land for a place to call our own. When we discovered a secluded area, Natalie worked her technological wizardry, constructing a smart mansion integrated seamlessly into the network. The result was a technological marvel, a testament to Natalie's ingenuity that left us in awe.

As my god-like followers flocked together, recruiting others during our wanderings, tales of my feats rippled through the land. The stories echoed the reality of how I closed the rift in the universe, saving the world from a nightmarish demise, albeit at the cost of a sacrifice.

A following emerged people drawn to witness my powers, some even willing to be sacrificed, believing it to be a gateway to paradise. Disturbed by this cult-like devotion, my initial god-like agents advised me to keep them for protection, and I, perhaps intoxicated by newfound power, heeded their counsel.

Enjoyment mingled with the power I held over others. The line blurred as I started to believe myself a god and my followers my subjects. The first eight loyalists earned the name "the body of god," a title that signaled a descent into a warped reality.

My personality took a darker turn—narcissism and egotism overshadowed the person I once was. Blame found a target in Dr. Creed, Alice, Elijah, and Maximus. In my skewed logic, their lack of sacrifice proved a betrayal. They had used me as a weapon, uncaring about the cost.

I transformed into a maniac, a god unaware of his madness. Settling into our new place with "the body of god," a sea of followers congregated in front of the smart mansion, waiting to be addressed by their proclaimed deity.

Stepping into the spotlight amid thunderous applause, "the body of god" flanking me, I unleashed a speech that bared the depths of my sanity.

"Welcome, my extraordinary assembly! Let's cut to the cosmic chase, folks. We're staring down the barrel of an existential shotgun, but fear not – Captain Cyrus, your cosmic guide, is here with the divine scoop.

Imagine this: the end of days, a cosmic cliffhanger on the brink. But rejoice! We've got the VIP pass to derail that apocalyptic train. How, you ask? Sacrifices, my fine folks – the ultimate key to the promised land. It's an honor, a choice, and tonight, we're putting it all on the sacrificial menu!"

The crowd erupted in ecstatic screams.

"Feel that energy? That's the symphony of allegiance – you guys are nailing it. Your devotion echoes like a cosmic rock concert, but, you know, the universe's version."

More cheers thundered through the assembly.

"Your cheers are the sweet serenade to my ears, a mask to the subtle unraveling within me. It's like a storm brewing under the surface – a mysterious force that even I can't fully comprehend. But who needs understanding when we have madness, right?

So, buckle up, my cosmic squad! We're hurtling into the divine chaos. This storm within me? It's our ticket to birthing something new, something godly. Sacrifice by sacrifice, we're crafting a masterpiece, transcending reality like the rebels of a cosmic revolution.

Let's fully embrace the unraveling – it's our wild ride into the promised land. Envision a realm where gods sculpt reality like master artists. Our cheers will echo through eternity, a testament to the wild power of divine madness.

And remember, dear followers, as we embark on this cosmic rollercoaster: "There are no accidents, just gods that hunger to be fed." Now, let's etch our mark on the tapestry of history!"

The assembly exploded in fervent devotion, solidifying their loyalty to their eccentric leader. The cheers acted as a veil, concealing the deepening turmoil within me—a shadowy tempest that churned unnoticed amidst the tumultuous aftermath of applause.

DR CREED

In the glow of my office, I poured over documents, the hum of computers underscoring my solitude. The past weeks had been a relentless pursuit to resurrect the program from the ashes left by the tournament's grim end. Alice, Elijah, and Maximus had been pillars of support, aiding in this arduous endeavor.

Yet, no amount of operational success could mask the somber reality. I found myself standing amidst godlike agents, mourning the fallen. The funeral held a weight of grief, and as we paid our respects, I couldn't shake the sense that the true loss wasn't in the victors of the tournament, but in Cyrus himself.

Alice, solemn and steadfast, provided updates on scouting missions searching for Cyrus. The elusive figure had become the epicenter of whispers, with cults emerging in various regions, each a distorted reflection of the man we once knew.

As I contemplated the daunting path that lay before us, the harsh truth loomed in the air like an unspoken decree – the defeat of Moros Noctis rested on the fractured unity of Cyrus, Maximus, Alice, and Elijah. It was a puzzle, with each crucial piece scattered across realms, awaiting assembly.

My mind drifted back to the day I first stumbled upon Cyrus Finch's file. It was a calculated move, orchestrating the intricacies that would lead him to descend into the supernatural world, all so I could take him under my wing. Little did I foresee the tragic death of his parents, and certainly not the heartbreaking loss of his sister. Yet, in the pursuit of an Inugami, even though the cost was exorbitant, the kingmaker did not disappoint in bestowing formidable power. The pieces were set in motion, with the realm of the supernatural intricately entwined with the human, forging a destiny none of us could escape.

Elijah's declaration of departure unfurled through the room, the weight of his promise to Cyrus hanging on each carefully chosen word. A solemn quite followed, broken by Alice's revelation.

As Elijah stood there, he unraveled the details of his departure, the solemn oath he had made to Cyrus. He spoke of the pact, a promise that if Cyrus dared to take the life of another agent, Elijah would be the harbinger of his end. The gravity of the commitment echoed in the room, leaving an indelible mark on the air.

In the midst of the charged atmosphere, Alice stepped forward, her voice carrying the weight of a confession. She admitted to advising Cyrus to employ the Inugami, an act born from desperation to curb the potential destruction that might have ensued if Cyrus wielded his absolute command. The room absorbed the intricacies of the revelation, a web of decisions that now hung heavy, shaping the fate of their turbulent journey.

"Why, Alice?" Maximus questioned, a mix of betrayal and confusion etched across his face.

In a moment where the air was thick with emotion, Alice began to unravel the reasoning behind her choices. "Cyrus would have died if he used his absolute command," she explained, her words a fragile shield against the rising storm of judgment.

Elijah's anger erupted like a tempest. "Everyone dies. We put our lives on the line every second. What makes Cyrus any different?" he bellowed, his frustration reverberating through the room.

Maximus, his brows furrowed, added his voice to the tumult. "What about our agents in the medical bay? Did their lives not matter as much as Cyrus?"

With a heavy exhale, Alice's eyes, a storm of sorrow and determination, found Maximus's gaze. "Every life holds weight, Maximus, but in that moment, I couldn't see any other way to close the rift, and I was afraid that whatever came out of it was going to kill us all," she poured out, her voice a fragile melody echoing the gravity of decisions forged in the searing crucible of their challenges.

In the midst of this emotional confession, her gaze met Elijah's eyes, seething with fury.

Elijah, unyielding, reasoned "As far as I'm concerned, Cyrus's hands aren't the only ones stained with the blood of our agents."

The room descended into an uneasy quiet, Maximus and I ensnared in the turmoil of conflicting emotions. Desperation etched across her face, Alice cast her gaze around, searching for any glimmer of understanding and support.

In a moment etched with poignant vulnerability, she wove an illusion—a sunlit field adorned with blossoming flowers. Stepping into this ephemeral haven, she abruptly severed the connection, vanishing into the sanctuary she had crafted.

A heavy sigh escaped me, recognizing the departure of another comrade. Duty, unyielding, demanded my continued pursuit.

As the echoes of her departure lingered, I declared, "We're going to employ our best telepaths to uncover Cyrus Finch and his cults," unveiling a dual-faceted strategy. Team A would engage Cyrus directly, while additional teams struck at marked locations to erode his strength.

Maximus and Elijah immersed themselves in the intricate details, assigning roles for the impending mission. Elijah, a formidable force, would confront Cyrus head-on, providing a crucial distraction, while Maximus and I took on the formidable task of dismantling the largest cult nest.

Days passed, the plan evolving with each discussion. The telepaths scoured the world, uncovering the hidden locations of cult followers sprawled across the map. However, locating Cyrus proved challenging, as Rachel's formidable resistance thwarted the telepaths' attempts.

In the control room, monitors illuminated with the highlighted markers of various cult bases. Standing alongside Maximus and Elijah, we observed the screens showcasing the dispersed nests of fanatical followers.

I turned to Maximus and Elijah; determination etched across my face. "Do it."

Maximus and Elijah synchronized their powers, conjuring a devastating combination move known as "Celestial Havoc." Maximus summoned meteors from the heavens, and with Elijah's touch, the celestial rocks gained sentience, enabling them to navigate with precision and lock onto their designated targets. All of this unfolded within the confines of the control room.

The monitors flickered as the combined forces of Maximus and Elijah executed their devastating assault. In a flash, the highlighted cult locations blinked off the map, leaving only the residue of their eradication. The mission was an unequivocal success, and the telepaths continued their work, pinpointing additional bases for Elijah and Maximus to eliminate.

However, amid the triumph, a sudden change seized Elijah's face with palpable fear, casting a foreboding shadow over the room.

""What's the matter?" I asked, my curiosity laced with concern.

Elijah, struggling to articulate his distress, mumbled about losing touch with someone. Frustration etched Maximus's face as I pressed for a more detailed explanation. Elijah, burdened, confessed to feeling the life force of people—a skill with its boundaries.

"Why not use it on Cyrus?" I pressed; my voice tinged with urgency.

"Dr. Creed, you warned me against forming close bonds due to the dangers of potential sacrifice. We treated him like a mark, just as you advised," Elijah explained. There was a pause, a heavy breath before he continued, "But in doing so, I fear we might have inadvertently pushed him down the path of destruction."

In my overconfidence, I might have unwittingly unleashed yet another formidable force.

Elijah dropped a bombshell, shattering the fragile equilibrium of our gathering. His words echoed through the room like an ominous refrain — he could no longer feel the life force of Alice. A chilling silence descended, the gravity of his revelation settling like a heavy fog. Maximus, caught in the haunting realization, stood frozen, his eyes betraying a mix of shock and fear.

The weight of the moment hung in the air, threatening to suffocate us with its implications. As I sought to grasp the magnitude of Elijah's revelation, the mission's importance became secondary to the personal toll it exacted. The very core of our unity seemed to splinter, the bonds that held us together fraying with each passing heartbeat.

In an attempt to pull Elijah back from the precipice of despair, I implored, my voice laden with both concern and urgency. However, his response was a defiant laughter that cut through the heavy air like a sharp blade. With a determined stride, he stepped into a rift of his own creation, disappearing from our midst.

The fractured allegiance now hung in the room like a tapestry of emotions, intricate and tangled. Duty beckoned us forward, but the personal cost of sacrifice lingered, threatening to tear us apart from within. Each step towards the mission carried the weight of uncertainty, the unspoken fear that the path we tread might lead us further into the shadows of our own making.

CYRUS FINCH

I stood upon the floating base, a god overlooking the devoted sea of followers who looked to me with reverence. The echoes of miracles and sacrifices resonated in the air, each act solidifying my ascendancy. The world was a canvas, painted with the strokes of my divine influence. Sarah, Ethan, Mason, Lily, James, Natalie, Gavin, and Rachel—each held a fragment of my essence, entrusted to safeguard and govern, spread across distant corners of the world.

Yet, amidst the celestial symphony, an unexpected discord pierced the divine atmosphere. A significant number of followers, like flickering stars, disappeared simultaneously. The devoted sea, once united in their unwavering connection to me, exhibited a disconcerting rupture. A wave of collective silence replaced the harmonious hum of devotion, casting a shadow over the divine landscape. As their life forces blinked out, the loss of their existence mirrored the extinguishing of lives, leaving an unsettling void in the tapestry of my godly dominion.

As the echoes of their absence reverberated through the sanctum, a hesitant knock on the door disrupted the divine solitude. Intrigued and somewhat apprehensive, I opened the door to find several of my followers standing outside, their faces a blend of uncertainty and reverence.

"Lord Cyrus," one of them spoke, the usual unwavering devotion now tinged with a subtle hesitation. "We felt a disturbance, a disconnection, and feared the worst. Something has transpired in the celestial realms."

To my astonishment, they entered not with the usual reverence but with Alice in chains, her once-familiar eyes now filled with a mixture of defiance and resignation.

"Lord Cyrus, she turned herself in, seeking you out.

The air was laden with unspoken emotions as Alice, in a rare display of vulnerability, began to apologize for her role in the deaths of the agents. She urged me to return, expressing a profound sense of loss. Her words hung in the air, each syllable a delicate note in the melody of our complex history.

"I didn't foresee the tragedy that befell our agents," Alice confessed, her eyes reflecting a mixture of guilt and genuine regret. "But we need you, Cyrus. The world needs you. I need you."

I observed her carefully, weighing the sincerity of her words against the echoes of our shared past. Alice had been both a confidante and a betrayer, a complex presence in the tapestry of my existence. As she spoke, the dance of emotions intensified, an intricate choreography of remorse and yearning.

"There was a time when your name held a different weight for me," I responded, my voice measured. "But the past cannot be undone. The sacrifices have been made, and my path is set."

The room seemed to hold its breath as Alice, her eyes shimmering with unshed tears, reached out. Her hand hovered in the space between us, a tentative bridge to a time when our connection held a different resonance. The unspoken words hung heavy, a silent plea for reconciliation.

"I can't change what has happened, Cyrus," Alice whispered, her voice a fragile echo in the vastness of the room. "But we can shape the future together. You have the power to make a difference, to lead with compassion and understanding."

The air crackled with tension as I considered her words. The weight of my godhood bore down on me, a responsibility I couldn't easily shed. The world had come to recognize me as a deity, and my influence had woven itself into the very fabric of reality.

"I am more than a man now," I replied, my tone carrying the weight of divinity. "The world has embraced my influence. The sacrifices, the miracles—they are the threads that bind me to a destiny greater than any mortal could fathom."

Alice's gaze held mine, a silent acknowledgment of the chasm that had grown between us. The dance continued, intricate steps leading us through the labyrinth of our shared history.

"The path I walk is one that transcends human bonds," I continued. "My followers look to me for guidance, for miracles. I have become something beyond the constraints of mortal emotions."

Her eyes, once filled with both warmth and betrayal, searched mine for a glimmer of the man she once knew. But the reflection staring back at her was that of a god, detached and resolute.

"I can't go back," I declared, a finality in my words. "My purpose lies in the destiny I've forged. I am their god, and they need me."

The room settled into a heavy silence, the echoes of our conversation lingering in the air like a poignant melody. The dance between Alice and me had reached its crescendo, a poignant moment frozen in the annals of time.

As she turned to leave, a trace of resignation in her posture, I felt a twinge of something indescribable. It was a fleeting moment, a whisper of the past that threatened to unravel the carefully constructed tapestry of my godhood. But I couldn't allow sentiment to sway my purpose.

"Come back, Alice," I beckoned. She turned, and I seized her hand with the authority of one who believes in the absolute power of their will. An impulse guided by divine entitlement.

In that moment, an illusion unfolded around us, a manifestation of Alice's creativity under my divine influence. Colors, ideas, paintings, universes—all carefully curated to reflect the magnificence of my godhood. The tapestry she wove was breathtaking, a mere reflection of the grandeur I envisioned as a deity.

As the illusion abruptly unraveled, my arms moved mechanically, compelled by an unseen force, a macabre dance orchestrated by cosmic strings. The transition from the enchanting illusion to stark reality was abrupt. My hands, once cloaked in the illusion's splendor, now dripped with Alice's blood. The blade I held descended relentlessly, fueled by an unforgiving rage that tolerated no resistance. In the midst of this turmoil, I repeated the word "Die" with each brutal thrust, my voice interwoven with the gruesome cadence of my actions. Simultaneously, invoking the inugami curse heightened the cosmic tension. The blade twisted in my grasp, and the relentless repetition of "Die" punctuated the air, creating a chilling symphony of finality. In my callous dismissal, I thrust Alice away like a discarded plaything, the culmination of my assault resulting in an explosive burst that ripped her body in half. The room, once emblematic of my godly ascendancy, now bore witness to a tableau of grotesque brutality.

Yet, as I implored my followers for help, the chilling truth dawned—they were already dead, sacrificed to the inugami for my merciless act of killing Alice.

Before I could grasp the gravity of what had just unfolded, a surge of energy filled the room, crackling with the intensity of a god's fury. A ripple opened, and Elijah emerged, his words thundering through the sanctum. "Cyrus! What have you done?" The reckoning had arrived, and in my realm, the confrontation with Elijah marked the inception of a divine trial.

   The divine sanctum, now tainted by the lingering scent of blood and haunted by the echoes of Alice's shattered illusion, transformed into the battleground for a reckoning that surpassed mortal comprehension. Elijah's accusatory gaze bore into mine, a challenge to the very core of my godhood. The room, once a symbol of divine power, now stood as a canvas for the clash between God and man, awaiting the ominous consequences of my actions.

DR CREED

In the celestial theater of our cosmic mission, Maximus and I collaborated with the most formidable telepaths the godlike project had to offer, aiming to unveil the concealed nests of Cyrus's cult. Our strategy unfolded intricately – dispatching teams through the globe to extinguish the vulnerable humans, ensnared by the deceptive allure of Cyrus's blessings.

Yet, at the core of our plan lay the strategic focus on the "Body of God," the high priests embedded in Cyrus's cult. A clandestine conversation between Maximus and me unfolded, a pact born out of necessity to confront each of the eight priests unitedly. The ever-present threat of Ethan's elusive speed added urgency, shaping our plan to tackle every priest together to minimize the risk.

As the celestial chessboard of our battle unfolded, the revelation of Lily's whereabouts surfaced. Maximus and I located her, safeguarding a stronghold buzzing with devoted cult followers. Before Lily could greet Maximus with deceptive innocence, a sudden distortion in the fabric of reality occurred. James emerged from a portal; urgency etched across his face.

"Lily, the doctor is here to kill you. I barely escaped my death," James exclaimed, recounting the harrowing details of his escape. His warning hung in the air; a crucial message delivered just moments before Lily's seemingly innocent greeting.

A fleeting exchange of glances sparked the question: "Lily or James?" I turned to Maximus, who chuckled, asserting, "She wields god's literal strength. She's mine." With a nod, our roles were defined.

Turning my attention to James, I enveloped myself in Tengoku's aura, delving into Jikan's abilities to master the manipulation of time. A fragment of Jikan split into my consciousness as I adorned his cloak of power, preparing for the cosmic clash that awaited.

In the silence preceding the cosmic tempest, the clash erupted between the four celestial fighters. Lily, Maximus, James, and I became cosmic dancers, weaving through the fabric of reality with our godlike abilities.

Amidst the cosmic battleground, Maximus, clad in a newly forged armor of omni-kinetic construct, faced the formidable force that was Lily. The celestial clash unfolded with a symphony of elemental chaos, each strike resonating with godly power.

As James and I delved into our own temporal dance, traversing through time portals, the novice attempts of James to engage me paled in comparison to Jikan's seasoned mastery. I deftly evaded his frustrated onslaught, my focus honed on the cosmic confrontation between Maximus and Lily.

The engagement reached a crescendo as Maximus, fortified in his omni-kinetic armor, stood against the onslaught of Lily's celestial might. Her strength shredded through the armor, a testament to the overwhelming power she wielded.

In a display of sheer power, Maximus summoned lightning bolts from the cosmic expanse, directing their ferocity towards Lily. Unfazed, she deftly caught the celestial lightning, molding it with her godlike strength into a spear of pure energy.

The cosmic ballet continued, with Maximus adapting his strategy. Recognizing that close combat was not an option against Lily's might, he unleashed a barrage of elemental attacks – bolts of lightning, waves of fire, gusts of wind – all aimed at Lily from various directions.

Nimble and strategic, Lily avoided the onslaught, deflecting and countering with the celestial spear she had fashioned. The battlefield crackled with the clash of elemental forces, each movement a testament to the godly power at play.

While the cosmic duel unfolded, James, in a misguided attempt to seize an opportunity, attacked me. Swiftly, I opened a portal to the ancient past, unleashing a T. rex into the present. The ensuing chaos echoed with the screams of a frost-crunching bite before the time portal sealed, a stark reminder of the hierarchy of our creation.

Maximus and Lily's cosmic confrontation pressed on. Lily, relentless in her pursuit, sought to close the distance, but Maximus, displaying tactical brilliance, continued his assault from a distance. Elements clashed, and the battleground transformed into a cosmic arena, each movement a dance of power and strategy.

As the celestial battle raged, the dynamics between Maximus and Lily became increasingly intricate. Lily's relentless strength, coupled with years of training, posed a challenge that even Maximus hadn't fully anticipated. The cosmic showdown, a tapestry woven with elemental fury, unfolded with the weight of godly power at stake.

In the cosmic clash between Maximus and Lily, the battlefield resonated with the power of gods. As Lily closed the distance, her attacks carried the force of the Big Bang, each blow striking Maximus with overwhelming celestial might.

Tension gripped the air with each blow, my instincts urging intervention, yet a deeper realization held me back. In that moment of peril, I understood the necessity of this trial by cosmic fire. Maximus, battered and tense, faced the onslaught of Lily's godlike prowess, his every move a struggle against the might of an ascendant deity.

As the battle reached its climax, Lily's small form proved to be her greatest asset, granting her unparalleled speed and nimbleness. Maximus fought valiantly, attempting to evade and counter Lily's onslaught, but the tide turned against him.

My eyes widened in shock as Lily, with a swift and devastating motion, extended her fist into Maximus's chest. The resulting explosion was horrific, and I stood there frozen, regret coursing through me for not intervening when the cosmos hung in a delicate balance.

In a sudden surge of energy, Maximus coughed, his form transcending the boundaries of mortality. "Kinetic Ascendance" unfurled its cosmic spectacle, transforming Maximus into a living conduit of kinetic energy. Strands of ethereal energy intertwined with his being, creating an iridescent aura that pulsated with the heartbeat of cosmic forces.

In this godlike state, Maximus gained the ability to manipulate kinetic energy at a level beyond mortal comprehension. He became a walking nexus of power, bending reality itself to his will. Every movement resonated with the harmonies of kinetic forces, distorting the fabric of space-time with each stride.

The transformation marked Maximus's ascent to the divine echelons of existence. "Kinetic Ascendance" had not only saved him from defeat but propelled him into the pantheon of deities. As he strode through the realms, his footsteps echoed with the resonance of omnipotent kinetic might, leaving an indelible mark on the cosmic tapestry. The battle had birthed a god, and the universe would feel the ripples of his newfound omnipotence.

CYRUS FINCH

Within the sacred confines of my divine sanctum, Elijah and I embroiled ourselves in a visceral conflict, a cosmic ballet resonating with the tempestuous forces that defined our godly existence. The initial clash unfolded as a raw exhibition of physical might, a brutal interplay that showcased Elijah's superior training, rendering me disarmed and at his mercy. Each strike and throw served as a testament to his martial mastery.

My divine commands, authoritative proclamations that should have held sway, were met with an unyielding onslaught. Elijah's martial finesse imposed a brutal silence, turning my divine decrees into futile echoes. The confrontation, escalating in ferocity, transitioned into a grand spectacle of godly powers. The once-hallowed sanctum transformed into a theater of elemental pandemonium, each unleashed force contributing to the chaotic dance of our cosmic struggle.

I beckoned forth tornadoes that twisted the very air, unleashed torrents of flames that danced in chaotic elegance, and conjured thunderstorms whose roars echoed my absolute command at its zenith. Yet, Elijah, an embodiment of resilience and cunning, deftly navigated through the elemental chaos, countering every ferocious manifestation with a survival instinct honed through rigorous training.

The pivotal moment dawned when Elijah unfurled the full breadth of his dominance. Beyond an ordinary godlike being, he manifested as a primordial force, a creation of the godlike project wielding the very essence of reality-shaping power. His supremacy transcended the conventional bounds of godhood, tapping into the core of creation itself.

In the unfolding tapestry of our divine clash, Elijah and I waged a fierce war of reality manipulation. I, commanding the fabric of existence, found myself a witness to Elijah's audacious rewriting and the birth of entirely new dimensions. His creativity defied my divine decrees, turning our confrontation into a cosmic ballet of omnipotent forces.

In a last-ditch effort to assert my godhood, I summoned my inugami, a mythical demon dog materializing by my side. The once-hallowed sanctum, a symbol of my divine ascendancy, transformed into the arena of a divine inquisition, where Elijah's accusatory gaze challenged the very core of my god complex, and the repercussions of our celestial confrontation loomed ominously in the charged atmosphere of the divine sanctum.

I unleash the inugami into the cosmic battleground, commanding the mythical beast to strike at Elijah with unbridled ferocity. Each command is a divine decree, an attempt to tear apart the elusive godlike being that dance with unnatural grace, dodging the relentless onslaught.

My scream, filled with a seething hatred for Elijah, echoes through the divine sanctum. The frigid tendrils of emotion course through my veins as I commanded him to "die." Outside, a group of my loyal followers pays the price, exploding into oblivion. Yet, my focus swiftly returns to the inner sanctum, where Elijah, reduced to a shower of visceral remnants, undergoes an instant rebirth mid-motion. The force of his punch sends me hurtling backward, only to rise again, fueled by celestial determination.

Elijah's voice cuts through the cosmic chaos, anger resonating as he accuses, "So you're attempting to end me?" Undeterred, he readies for the next assault, and in a surge of fear-driven desperation, I unleash a torrent of screams. Each fervent plea for his demise carries the cold pulse of malevolence, and the sacrifice of my followers intensifies.

Chilling sensations surge through my veins as the dark curse exact its toll. Elijah, unfazed by the recurrent detonations, resurfaces relentlessly. With each revival, he closes the distance, resuming his onslaught. The divine sanctum transforms into a battleground, resonating with celestial echoes as I engage in a desperate dance, making Elijah explode repeatedly to momentarily halt his relentless advances.

The eerie cadence of demise reverberates through the divine sanctum, a haunting testament to the price paid in my desperate bid to thwart the enraged godlike entity. Sacrificing followers in this celestial game, I navigate the shifting tides of battle, seeking a momentary reprieve from Elijah's relentless pursuit.

DR CREED

As Maximus surveyed the battlefield, a tranquil confidence exuded from his every movement. Lily, a seemingly insignificant entity in his cosmic calculations, faced the first wave of his godly manipulation. Shackles materialized around her wrists and feet with but a mere thought, a testament to Maximus's absolute control over the ethereal realm.

His voice echoed in my mind, as though he stood right beside me. "Things are about to get crazy. Don't intervene," Maximus declared, acknowledging my distant presence as the cosmic spectacle unfolded.

Lily, however, defied the ethereal constraints, veins bulging with the surge of godlike strength. With a forceful break, she shattered the ethereal shackles. Maximus, unperturbed, divided himself into seven duplicates, a celestial mirage that marked the beginning of his intricate strategy.

"Subdue them, don't kill the priest," Maximus commanded as he propelled six of his duplicates into different portals, dispatching them on specific missions while leaving the gateways open for their return.

In a swift lunge, Lily closed the distance, her attacks a flurry of blows landing with precision upon Maximus's celestial form. The air around them began to crackle with the intensity of their otherworldly clash.

Without a visible motion, Maximus released an aura, creating a 500-meter ethereal boundary. The world outside this celestial arena remained untouched, shielding the mortal realm from the tempest within. Finally, Maximus, having observed Lily's relentless assault, chose to engage.

In the midst of the cosmic turmoil, Maximus, enveloped in the radiance of "Kinetic Ascendance," unleashed a calculated surge of kinetic energy. The shockwave sent Lily hurtling backward, breaking through the ethereal barrier that had contained their titanic clash. My gaze followed Maximus, who, with a glance at the portals, revealed a more intricate plan in motion.

Observing the portals, I noticed they opened to six different locations, each depicting a fierce confrontation between Maximus and the enigmatic "Body of God." My attention focused on the closest portal, revealing Maximus engaged in an intricate dance of power with Sarah. It became evident that Maximus was showcasing the stark disparity between their understanding of power, reducing Sarah's formidable abilities to a mere droplet compared to his ocean of knowledge.

As Lily returned to the fray, she locked into combat with Maximus, who, with an almost playful demeanor, allowed her to get dangerously close. His choice to employ hands instead of the mere thought-driven use of power showcased a deliberate effort to make the battle more engaging.

In a dance of divine forces, Maximus countered Lily's barrage with calculated precision. Each movement and strike echoed with the harmonies of celestial power. The cosmic arena became a canvas for their godly clash, a spectacle that defied mortal comprehension.

The ethereal boundary pulsated with the crescendo of their battle, and Maximus, no longer passive, unleashed a torrent of divine energy, pushing back against Lily's overwhelming strength. The cosmic symphony of their clash unfolded with an intensity that transcended the boundaries of mere mortal combat.

Amidst the celestial chaos, Lily harnessed the godly might bestowed upon her, focusing it into a devastating move known as "Celestial Cataclysm." Her fists, empowered by divine strength, became the epicenter of destruction as she unleashed a concentrated strike. The celestial energy surged, creating a shockwave that threatened to shatter barriers and wreak havoc within the confined arena.

My attention shifted to the next portal, revealing a Maximus clone emerging with the unconscious form of Mason. The situation grew even more dire as screams echoed from three different portals. Each displayed Maximus decimating entire compounds housing the "Body of God," showcasing a devastating power that surpassed mere subduing.

Returning to the central battle, Maximus and Lily continued their intense engagement. Beyond the wild, breaking battle, I could sense Maximus investing more than mere playfulness. There was a mutual respect for Lily's combat prowess and power. It seemed Maximus not only faced her as a formidable adversary but also derived enjoyment from the challenging duel.

In a sudden swish, Sarah was thrown out of a portal, followed by a Maximus clone escorting her unconscious form. All portals closed after a loud explosion erupted from them, except one, which revealed Ethan stepping out.

In the unfurling cosmic tapestry, Maximus' transformation reached heights beyond my comprehension. An awareness emanated from him that transcended mere senses, instantaneously detecting Ethan's arrival, even without visible cues. The scattered clones returned to him as he adjusted his focus.

Maximus' demeanor underwent a profound shift as he allowed Lily's ultimate move to strike him squarely in the chest—a blow that would have been fatal for most godlike beings. However, Maximus not only shrugged it off, but he also posed a question to Lily, a question laden with the weight of his authority over kinetic energy. "You know I wrote laws for kinetic energy, right?"

The godlike agent unleashed all the kinetic energy he had accumulated, a pulsating wave emanating from his form, responding to the onslaught of Lily's attacks, which were enhanced by the very strength of gods. In a cataclysmic display, Lily was atomized, and the ethereal barrier spared the world from experiencing a cosmic detonation akin to the Big Bang.

Ethan, witnessing this unfathomable event, screamed in protest as he sped toward the barrier. "No!"

Maximus, reveling in his godlike state, chuckled at Ethan's futile attempt. "You should've stayed out of this barrier. Now I can kick your ass without worrying about reality."

With a mere thought, Maximus closed the barrier, trapping them in a cosmic battleground. His eyes, now celestial storms, glowed with an intensity that bespoke a power beyond mortal comprehension.

Maximus cracked his neck, a chilling smile playing on his lips. "Alice was a friend of mine," he mused, his voice resonating with an unearthly echo. "I want you to go all out."

Ethan attempted a confident smile, but the realization dawned upon him, and even I could sense the magnitude of what unfolded. Maximus's eyes and aura transformed into forces of celestial might that surpassed anything I had ever encountered. "If I go all out, the world ends," Ethan confessed.

"Don't worry about that. You won't live to see tomorrow. Besides, you didn't care about that when you took out Ashley," Maximus declared, sending a pulsating wave of energy around himself.

In that moment, the voice of Jikan echoed in my mind. "You're going to need to slow time down to a stop if you wish to witness your prodigy fight."

The clash between Maximus and Ethan unfolded at literal godspeed, a realm beyond the perception of any mere mortal. As they blurred through the arena, I questioned whether I, too, would be able to witness this ethereal confrontation without the guidance of the eight kitsunes possessing my soul. The celestial battle surged, each move resonating with the echoes of godly power, a spectacle that danced on the edge of time itself.

The celestial clash between Maximus and Ethan unfolded within the confines of the barrier, preventing the catastrophic consequences their godspeed battle threatened. Laws governing Godspeed fights were pushed to the brink, the very fabric of reality bending and warping under the sheer force they exerted.

The 500-meter barrier defied the laws of physics, containing a universe within its confines, a realm where Maximus wielded divine authority. The transformed Maximus utilized this self-contained world to combat Ethan, his godlike speed an overwhelming force that matched the laws he himself had written.

Despite the awe-inspiring spectacle, a lingering concern crept into my mind – the potential limitations of Maximus holding onto this godly form. The battle of fists, kicks, and parries thrown at Godspeed continued relentlessly within the cosmic arena.
As the godlike clash raged on, I couldn't help but be grateful for Maximus's foresight in creating the barrier. The battle seemed to extend for ages, and my attention shifted briefly to the last open portal, revealing a surviving faction of the cult.

In an instant, I navigated through the portal, arriving in a dense forest. The larger cult nest was hidden in a bunker, and I summoned all my kitsunes – Jikan, Kasai, Kaze, Ongaku, Chiyku, Sanda, Seishen, Kukan – to my side.

"Let's finish and get back to Maximus," I declared, anticipating the mission ahead. Jikan, however, questioned the righteousness of our actions. With a sigh, I emphasized our mission: to save Cyrus and keep Elijah alive.

With a unanimous decision, the nine tails unleashed their elemental forces, combining fire, lightning, wind, earth, souls, shadow, sound, and time into a devastating bolt of light. The energy struck down, atomizing everything in its path, including the bunker.

Stepping back through the portal just in time, I marveled at the ongoing battle within the godlike speed barrier, where Maximus and Ethan continued their relentless clash at a pace that defied mortal perception.

In the celestial arena, the godspeed battle between Maximus and Ethan reached its peak. Ethan's movements blurred, a whirlwind of rapid strikes, kicks, and parries, showcasing unparalleled speed. In his transformed state, Maximus entered the cosmic ballet, deciphering the intricate patterns of Ethan's godspeed.

Seizing a strategic moment, Maximus's eyes locked onto the kinetic energy dance of Ethan's godspeed. With swift precision, he absorbed the essence of Ethan's rapid maneuvers. The celestial battlefield crackled as Ethan's godspeed, once formidable, now fueled Maximus's power.

The absorbed kinetic energy surged through Maximus, amplifying the ethereal storm around him. Celestial power resonated, and with newfound speed and resilience, Maximus closed the distance in an instant. In a dazzling display, he defied godspeed's laws, slowing time itself.

The arena transformed into a surreal dance. Ethan's once-blistering movements now appeared sluggish. Maximus, with a smirk, effortlessly danced around him, fixing his hair and straightening his shirt. His every move countered Ethan's attacks with deliberate precision.

The celestial ballet continued with Maximus narrating his actions, predicting Ethan's futile attempts. Each movement channeled the absorbed godspeed energy into devastating blows. Overwhelmed, Ethan struggled to match Maximus's newfound might.

In a symphony of celestial power, Maximus toyed with Ethan, showcasing disdain. The cosmic echoes marked Maximus's victory. Amidst the remnants of their godspeed battle, Maximus, a godlike force of kinetic ascendancy, asserted dominance over the celestial realm.

In a blinding display of celestial speed, Maximus launched an onslaught of strikes upon Ethan, each blow delivered with an otherworldly velocity that left trails of ethereal storms in its wake. The celestial arena became a canvas for their godspeed combat, where movements transcended mortal comprehension.

Ethan, once the master of godspeed, struggled to keep up with the celestial whirlwind that was Maximus. Strikes landed with the force of cosmic tempests, creating afterimages that danced in the wake of their godlike clash. The symphony of their battle echoed through the celestial expanse.

Maximus, a kinetic force at the peak of godspeed, continued the rapid assault, a relentless storm of blows that defied the laws of the celestial realm. The blinding pace of their combat painted a picture of celestial chaos, with Maximus reigning as the god of kinetic ascendancy.

As the celestial storm of Maximus's transformation reached its climax, a subtle shift occurred. The radiant aura that enveloped him began to wane, the iridescent threads of energy gradually fading away. The godlike brilliance that defined Maximus's kinetic ascendancy started to recede, marking the inevitable end of his transformative state.

In an unrelenting surge of godspeed, Maximus continued his celestial assault upon Ethan. Each strike was a blur, a cascade of divine force that left nothing but red mist in its wake. The celestial arena bore witness to the overwhelming power of kinetic ascendancy as Maximus pressed on, reducing Ethan to mere remnants of crimson haze.

In the wake of this celestial spectacle, Maximus returned to his mortal form, the echoes of godhood dissipating into the cosmic expanse. The once-glorious manifestation of kinetic ascendancy was replaced by a sense of temporal fragility, as the godlike powers that had defined the battlefield withdrew, leaving Maximus standing as a mortal once more.

Staring in shock, I fully grasped the magnitude of what stood before me. In my pursuit of godlike beings, I had inadvertently crafted gods. Maximus, in his transformed state, stood as a testament to the godlike power that surpassed mortal comprehension. The echoes of their celestial clash resonated in the divine realm, marking the creation of beings that transcended the boundaries of mere godhood.

CYRUS FINCH

Elijah's fists collided with me in a brutal display of physical might, the sheer impact echoing through the divine sanctum. Bones cracked, divine energy erupted, and the cosmic symphony of our clash reached a deafening crescendo. The sacred space became an arena of chaotic beauty, where every strike and counter echoed with the harmonies of celestial power.

In response to Elijah's relentless assault, I called upon the inugami, the mythical demon dog materializing with ethereal flames licking its fur. "Die!" I commanded, unleashing torrents of divine fire upon Elijah. The inferno danced and twisted; an otherworldly display of wrath aimed at the primordial force standing resilient amidst the celestial tempest.

Elijah's form flickered within the flames, an indomitable silhouette within the raging inferno. His punches, now intensified by the swirling flames, landed with thunderous force. I, fueled by the unwavering belief in my absolute command, met each strike with resilience. The sanctum transformed into a cosmic battleground, where the clash of our godly powers painted a tapestry of destruction and creation.

As the battle reached its zenith, desperation seized me. In an attempt to tip the scales, I invoked the dark curse, sacrificing followers to amplify the inugami's power. Explosions echoed through the sanctum, and Elijah, seemingly obliterated, reappeared in a shower of cosmic remnants. Yet, the cost on my once-loyal devotees weighed heavily on the cosmic scales.

Undeterred by the mounting toll, I persisted, relentlessly commanding the inugami to strike with unbridled ferocity. Each detonation sent shockwaves through the divine sanctum, tearing at the fabric of existence. Elijah, fueled by an unyielding determination, revised himself from cosmic dust, ready to continue his relentless assault.

The battlefield became a surreal dance of creation and annihilation. Elijah's reborn fists swung with primal force, and I, in response, fought back with the fervor of one who believed in his divine ascendancy. The sanctum's architecture crumbled under the cosmic pressure, and ethereal storms resonated with our godly might.

The struggle continued, each punch and explosion echoing through the celestial space. As the inugami's flames intertwined with Elijah's resilience, the battlefield became a cosmic forge, forging our conflict into a tale of celestial determination. The sanctum, once a symbol of divine ascendancy, now bore the scars of our relentless confrontation.

"Die," I commanded, and Elijah erupted into a cosmic spectacle of destruction. I took a breath, the icy sensation coursing through my veins as I enjoyed a fleeting moment of relaxation. But that moment was short-lived as Elijah reappeared above me, his fist descending with full force.

Swiftly, I dodged the impending strike, invoking the dark curse once more. The familiar chill swept through me, and I watched as Elijah exploded in a burst of cosmic remnants. "I can do this all day," I declared, determination resonating in my voice.

Elijah persisted, reviving each time with an unwavering resolve. "Die," I uttered, dodging another strike, and the cycle continued. "Die, dodge, die, dodge, die, die, die."

Amidst the relentless cosmic dance, Elijah's form flickered in and out of existence, each revival met by my unyielding determination. As explosions echoed through the divine sanctum, a strange conversation unfolded between us amid the chaos.

"You know," Elijah's voice cut through the chaos of our godly clash, "you bear the responsibility for the deaths of these agents, for Alice's demise."

As Elijah's accusing words reverberated through the cosmic tempest, his strikes became a relentless barrage, each blow carrying the weight of blame for the fallen agents and Alice's demise.

Dodging Elijah's strikes with calculated precision, I countered, my retort cutting through the explosive chaos surrounding us. "Your trust was never genuine. If it were, my inugami would've claimed three lives by now."

Despite the tumultuous explosions and chaos, Elijah's bitter chuckle echoed. "Cyrus, your understanding is skewed. Trust isn't measured in body counts. We believed in your vision, even when it demanded sacrifices."

Anticipating our clash, I readied myself to invoke the curse once more. Elijah's voice cut through the cosmic echoes as he delivered a profound truth. "This unending cycle won't erase the fact that we cared for you, Cyrus. The inugami's actions reflect the sacrifices we were willing to make for a greater purpose."

In the cosmic void, our confrontation reached a momentary pause. The sanctum, marred by the scars of our battle, bore witness to a celestial tapestry woven with accusations and unspoken realities. Our clash, entwined with creation and destruction, surpassed the limits of godly comprehension.

As the battle neared its zenith, the explosions harmonized with each curse invocation. Elijah, undeterred, rose from the cosmic remnants with unwavering determination. A storm of blows and divine reshaping painted the battlefield with ethereal hues, each punch etching its mark on my godly form.

My furious commands reverberated through the sanctum, "DIE! DIE! DIE!" A desperate attempt to assert control, to prove a point in the cosmic ballet of destruction. The divine clash reached a crescendo, our godly powers colliding with relentless force.

With every detonation, followers were sacrificed in desperate attempts to gain the upper hand. However, in the midst of the celestial struggle, a chilling realization dawned on me.

With desperate determination, I sought to summon the inugami once more. "Die!" I screamed, only to be met with resounding silence. The inugami, once a loyal servant, now stood dormant, indifferent to my commands.

Seizing the opportune moment, Elijah's fists descended with thunderous impact. My attempts to invoke the dark curse proved futile, the icy feeling eluding my grasp. The inugami, once a formidable force at my command, remained motionless—a silent observer to the culmination of our celestial struggle.

Gloating in his triumph, Elijah's voice echoed through the sanctum. "Your cult lies in ruins, Cyrus. You sacrificed everything, and yet, you stand alone."

As the words hung in the cosmic void, Elijah delivered a final, decisive blow. Darkness enveloped my consciousness as I succumbed to the overwhelming force of his strike.

The once-mighty godhood that I had wielded crumbled, leaving me defeated and unconscious amidst the remnants of our celestial battlefield. Elijah's gloating persisted in the silence that followed—a haunting reminder of the price paid for my misguided pursuit of transcendence.

DR CREED

Standing alongside Elijah and Maximus near the gravestone, the aftermath of the cosmic clash palpable, I pondered the twists of fate that had brought us here. Elijah, in the process of recovering his power over the past few days, reflected on Alice's predicament, expressing a wish that she had followed her dream of becoming a doctor.

In a moment of respite, I engaged Maximus in a conversation about his recent transformation. "Maximus, this newfound power is formidable, but its usage demands caution. We must ensure its wielded with precision to avoid unintended consequences. Balance is key," I advised, acknowledging the responsibility that came with such celestial abilities.

As we spoke, the ground beneath us began to vibrate, a subtle indication that the cosmic forces were still in flux. Recognizing the need for space, I informed Elijah and Maximus that I had to check on Cyrus, acknowledging the lingering complexities in the wake of our recent confrontations.

Descending into the compound, I found myself standing before the door that concealed Cyrus Finch. The room, an enigmatic sanctuary that held the remnants of our cosmic struggle, echoed with the weight of revelations and untold secrets. I took a deep breath, the air charged with the lingering essence of godly battles.

As the door creaked open, revealing the dimly lit space within, my eyes fell upon Cyrus. There he sat, absorbed in the act of writing, his focus unwavering as if the cosmic revelations had not shaken the very foundation of his existence. Ignoring my presence, he continued to etch words onto the pages before him.

"Cyrus," I addressed him, my voice cutting through the silence.

He glanced up, meeting my gaze with a mixture of apathy and curiosity. "What now, Dr. Creed?"

I stepped into the room, the cosmic residue clinging to the air. "You know, Cyrus, there's more to your story than you realize."

His eyes flickered with momentary interest, and he set aside his writing instrument. "Enlighten me, then."

I began to unravel the tapestry of his existence, each revelation a thread that wove together the intricate design of his purpose. "Moros Noctis wasn't just a threat. It was the reason you came into being, Cyrus. I created you to be a weapon, a tool to combat the darkness that threatened to consume us all."

Cyrus leaned back, his expression a mix of disbelief and skepticism. "So, I'm just a pawn in your grand design?"

"No," I corrected, my tone carrying a weight of sincerity. "You are the result of my attempt to save a life, to bring back Peter Wayne from the brink of death. Moros Noctis emerged from that experiment, and you were the answer to the darkness it unleashed."

The room seemed to shrink as the truth unfolded. "But why?" Cyrus questioned, his eyes narrowing.

"The inugami ritual, the dog cancer—I needed your skills and the inugami to defeat Moros Noctis," I explained. "And about the sacrifices, Cyrus, that was a fabrication."

His brows furrowed in confusion. "What do you mean? I've always needed sacrifices to use my powers."

I sighed, preparing to unveil the most profound revelation. "You never needed sacrifices, Cyrus. It was a psychological block, a twisted belief created to shield yourself from the truth."

He scoffed, dismissing my words. "That doesn't make sense. My parents died the first time I used my powers. I've always needed sacrifices."

I met his gaze, revealing a truth that had been concealed for far too long. "Your parents, Cyrus. That argument you had with them that morning—the neighbor who reported it to the police. You created a psychological block to shift the blame, to convince yourself that you needed sacrifices to use your powers. It was a coping mechanism to absolve yourself of the guilt."

The realization struck him like a celestial storm. His eyes widened, haunted by the weight of a truth he had long denied. "I killed my parents?"

"You were a person of interest in the investigation, but you were already at school when they died," I revealed. "You were never blamed because of that fabricated argument. Your powers were out of control, and you created a narrative to protect yourself."

Cyrus's mind grappled with the revelation, the pieces of his past falling into a horrifying place. "Alice... I killed her for nothing. She didn't die because she didn't care about me. She died because I was out of control."

A heavy silence enveloped the room as the truth settled in. I could see the torment in Cyrus's eyes, the realization of the lives lost, the relationships shattered, all based on a lie he had constructed.

"She did love you," I uttered, the words hanging in the air.

Staring directly into Cyrus's eyes, I voice my suspicions with a measured intensity.

"Cyrus, as I delved into your book, the tale you weave seems incongruent with the events that unfolded."

Cyrus responds with a casual shrug. "What's your point?"

Leaning in, I disclose a truth that could alter everything.

"Alice's illusions were powerless against me. If they persist for you, it raises a compelling possibility—Alice might still exist in a reality beyond our understanding."

I turned away, leaving Cyrus to confront the demons of his past. The door closed behind me, sealing the room that held the echoes of his revelation. As I walked away, thoughts swirled in my mind—thoughts of the war against Moros Noctis and the potential role Cyrus could still play.

The cosmic tapestry of our existence continued to weave intricate patterns, and in the aftermath of revelations, I knew that the battle was far from over. The door closed, leaving Cyrus Finch to face the truth within, and the cosmic struggle endured, reaching beyond the boundaries of godly comprehension.

SPEAK
"THE GRAPHIC NOVEL TEASER"

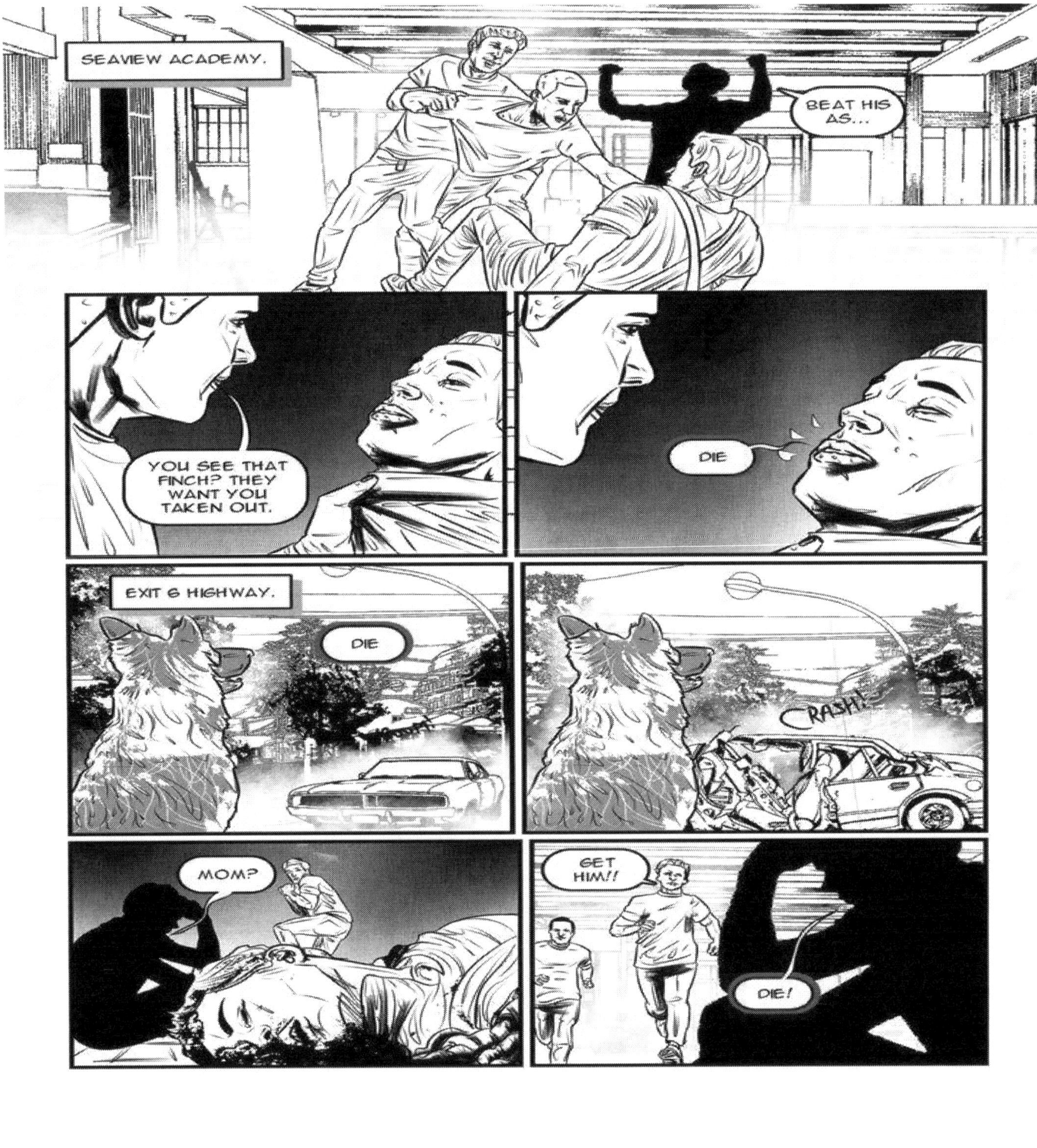
SEAVIEW ACADEMY.
BEAT HIS AS...
YOU SEE THAT FINCH? THEY WANT YOU TAKEN OUT.
DIE
EXIT 6 HIGHWAY.
DIE
CRASH!
MOM?
GET HIM!!
DIE!

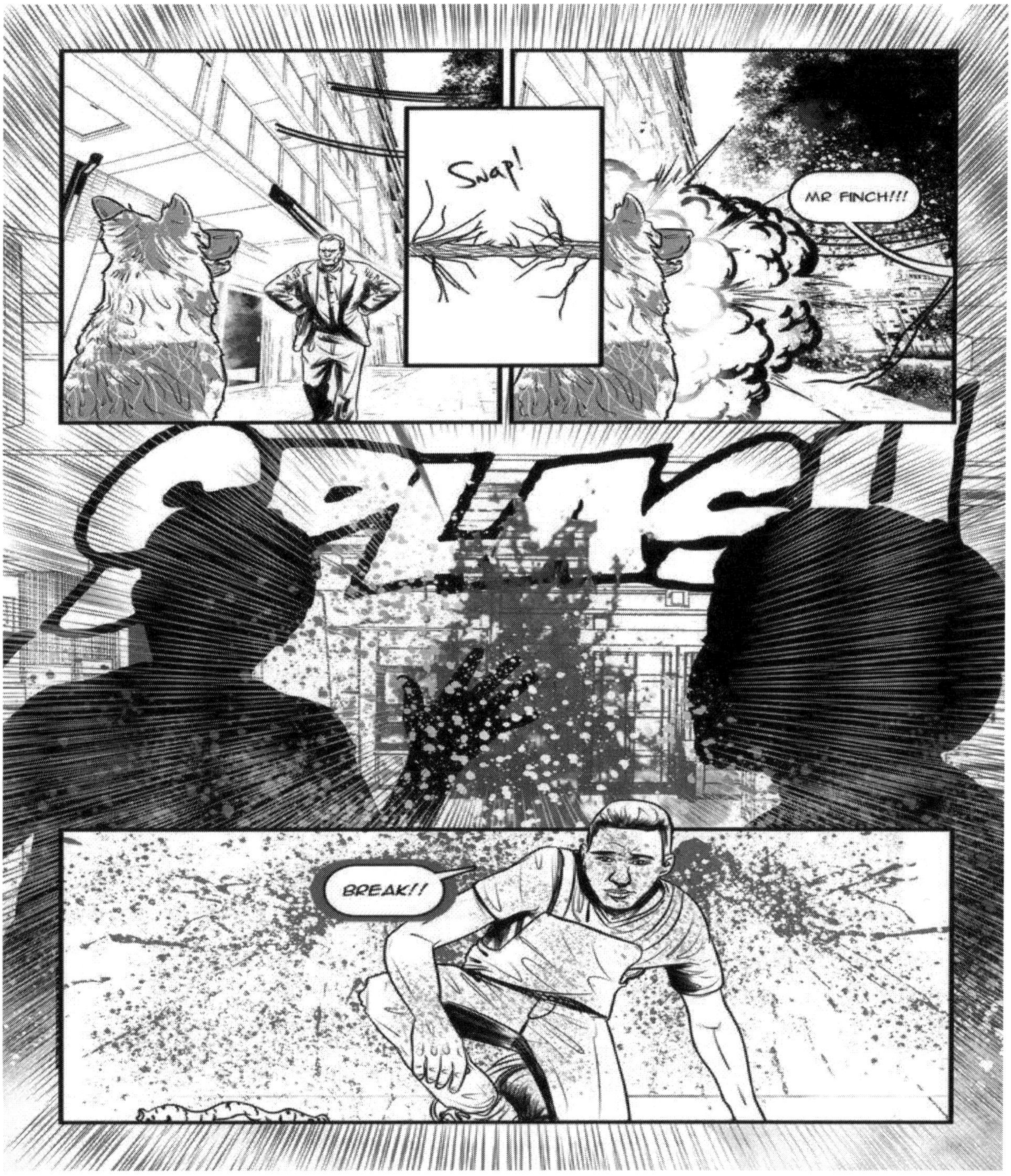
Snap!
MR FINCH!!!
BREAK!!

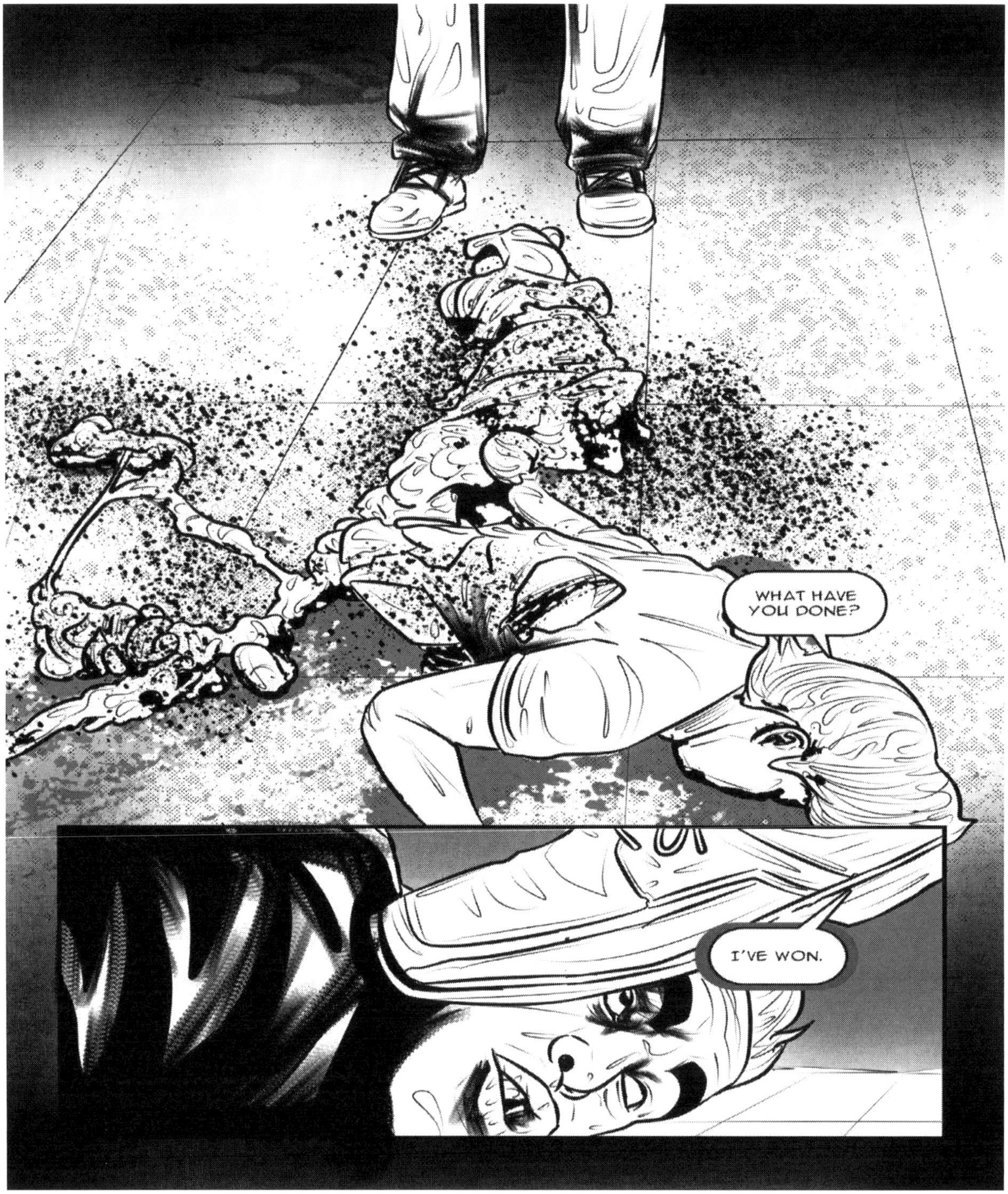
WHAT HAVE YOU DONE?
I'VE WON.

BUT IT DIDN'T HAVE TO BE THIS WAY.
IF I COULD GO BACK AND CHANGE WHAT I'VE DONE, I WOULD'VE SMASHED HIS BRAIN IN.

YOU ARE IN VIOLATION OF INTERNATIONAL LAW.
THINK THEY CAN TAKE US?
CAN GOD BE TAKEN DOWN BY A BULLET?
OPEN FIRE!!

163

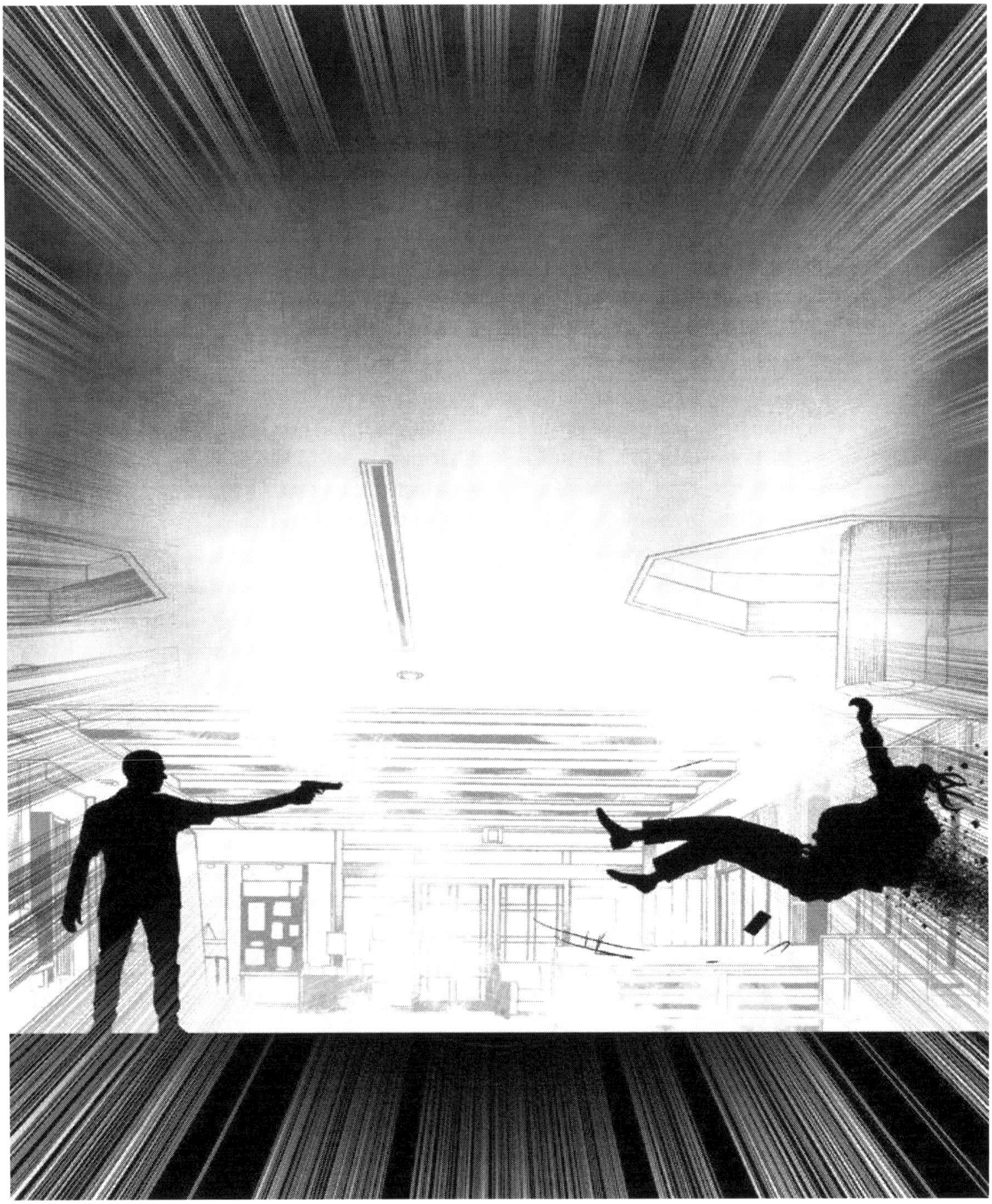

CHARACTERS

CYRUS FINCH

Character Bio: Cyrus Finch

Background:
Cyrus Finch, born on November 7th under the enigmatic Scorpio sign, carries the weight of a tumultuous past. Endowed with supernatural abilities, Cyrus is a complex individual navigating the thin line between power and morality.

Powers:
Cyrus wields the formidable gift of Absolute Command, allowing him dominion over celestial forces. This power, however, comes at a cost, feeding on his soul and stamina. In contrast, he commands the Inugami, a mythical demon dog, whose abilities demand sacrifices from those who care for him. This internal struggle forms the crux of Cyrus's journey.

Mental State:
Haunted by the consequences of his powers, Cyrus grapples with a fragile mental state. The burden of sacrificing others for strength weighs heavily on his conscience, adding layers of complexity to his character. His resilience is a testament to his internal strife, a constant battle between the desire for power and the moral repercussions of his actions.

Chase:
Driven by a mysterious force, Cyrus finds himself entangled in a chase that transcends the physical realm. Unraveling the secrets of his powers and their origin becomes his relentless pursuit. As he navigates this perilous journey, Cyrus confronts the manipulative influence of Dr. Creed, questioning his own existence and purpose in a world teetering on the brink of divine chaos.

Cyrus Finch, a Scorpio with celestial prowess, stands at the crossroads of destiny, seeking answers to the enigma of his powers while wrestling with the ethical quandaries that define his character.

DR CREED

Character Bio: Dr. Creed

Background:
Dr. Creed, born on December 22nd under the pragmatic Capricorn sign, emerges as a figure whose life intertwines the scientific and the supernatural. His journey unfolds against the backdrop of manipulating destinies and playing god with ancient powers.

Manipulative Brilliance:
Dr. Creed's brilliance extends beyond the laboratory, reaching into the intricate web of human lives. Gifted with the manipulative artistry of a puppeteer, he orchestrates the destinies of those around him, weaving a complex tapestry where science and divine forces dance in tandem.

Playing God:
The boundaries between scientist and deity blur as Dr. Creed grapples with the moral implications of his actions. Playing god with ancient powers, he navigates the delicate balance between innovation and responsibility, shaping the destinies of individuals to fulfill a vision of a world in peril.

Moral Dilemmas:
Dr. Creed's character is defined by the moral dilemmas he faces. The pursuit of scientific progress clashes with the consequences of manipulating lives, forcing him to confront the dualities of playing the role of both creator and destroyer in a world caught between tradition and innovation.

Chase of Power:
In the relentless chase for power and control, Dr. Creed's character unfolds against the backdrop of a narrative where manipulation becomes a means to an end. As he plays god with the lives of those around him, his own quest for understanding the supernatural forces within him adds layers to a character immersed in the pursuit of knowledge and dominance.

MAXIMUS

Character Bio: Maximus - The Omni-Kinetic Titan

Background:
Maximus, revered as one of the most formidable Godlike Agents, ascends to godhood through his unparalleled control over Omni-Kinetic energy. Born from the cosmic tapestry, Maximus stands as a Titan among celestial beings, a force of raw power and transformative might.

Omni-Kinetic Mastery
Maximus's command over Omni-Kinetic energy is unmatched, elevating him to the status of a cosmic deity. His ability to manipulate kinetic forces allows him to shape reality itself, making him a living embodiment of the fundamental energies that govern the universe.

Godlike Transformations:
In moments of celestial intensity, Maximus undergoes godlike transformations, transcending the limits of mortal comprehension. These metamorphoses turn him into a living god, a being whose very essence resonates with the cosmic forces he commands. Each transformation unveils a new facet of his godhood, marking him as a Titan in the pantheon of celestial entities.

Celestial Titan:
Maximus's status as a Celestial Titan stems not only from his Omni-Kinetic mastery but also from the profound impact of his presence in the cosmic narrative. His actions shape the destiny of the Godlike Agents, and his celestial might echo through the realms explored within the pages of "Speak."

Unparalleled Power:
Within the cosmic tapestry of "Speak," Maximus emerges as a beacon of unparalleled power. His every move reverberates through the celestial realms, leaving an indelible mark on the overarching narrative. Maximus's Godlike status sets him apart as a Titan whose power rivals the very forces that shape the cosmos.

Living Embodiment of Energy:
As the living embodiment of Omni-Kinetic energy, Maximus becomes a symbol of cosmic power and transformation. His journey within "Speak" unfolds as a testament to the immense influence wielded by a being whose essence is interwoven with the celestial energies that define the Godlike Agents' existence.

Cosmic Legacy:
Maximus's legacy extends beyond the pages of "Speak," becoming a cosmic imprint on the narrative. His journey, marked by godlike transformations and unmatched mastery, solidifies him as a Titan whose presence forever alters the destiny of the Godlike Agents within the expansive cosmic tapestry.

ELIJAH

Character Bio: Elijah - The Primordial Being

Background:
Elijah, a captivating presence among the Godlike Agents, emerges as a Primordial Being within the cosmic narrative of "Speak." His existence transcends conventional godhood, embodying the very essence of creation and reality-shaping power.

Primordial Force:
Unlike his fellow Godlike Agents, Elijah taps into a primordial force, a manifestation of the Godlike project's ambitious reach into the core of creation itself. His power extends beyond the ordinary, wielding reality-shaping abilities that redefine the boundaries of godhood.

Reality-Shaping Mastery:
Elijah's journey unfolds as a cosmic ballet of reality manipulation, where he commands the very fabric of existence. His mastery over shaping reality becomes a central theme, showcasing a level of creativity that defies the constraints of divine decrees, contributing to the intricate dance of omnipotent forces within "Speak."

Ambitious Creativity:
Within the tapestry of the divine clash, Elijah stands as a symbol of ambitious creativity. His audacious rewriting of reality births entirely new dimensions, marking him as a celestial architect whose powers challenge the status quo of Godlike Agents and the realms they traverse.

Godhood Redefined:
Elijah's presence challenges the conventional bounds of godhood, elevating him to a status beyond ordinary celestial beings. His journey within "Speak" becomes a testament to the limitless potential embedded in the Godlike project, where the lines between deity and creator blur.

Confrontation and Cosmic Ballet:
As the narrative unfolds, Elijah engages in a grand confrontation with his fellow Godlike Agents, particularly Cyrus. Their clashes become a cosmic ballet, a spectacular showcase of reality-shaping powers and the intricate dance of omnipotent forces that define their celestial struggle.

Legacy of Creation:
Elijah's legacy within "Speak" extends beyond the struggles of the Godlike Agents, leaving an indelible mark on the cosmic tapestry. His primordial influence, intertwined with the ambitious creativity of the Godlike project, reshapes the narrative, challenging the very fabric of existence and godly limitations.

ALICE

Character Bio: Alice - Weaver of Absolute Illusions

Background:
Alice, the mysterious newcomer in the cosmic saga of "Speak," weaves her enigmatic presence into the narrative with a past touched by war and an ability that transcends reality itself. Her role within the Godlike Agents unfolds as a key element in the cosmic tapestry of the unfolding story.

War-Touched Past:
Alice's brunette hair and eyes bear the silent stories of a life deeply affected by the ravages of war. The scars etched into her existence serve as a testament to the battles fought and the hardships endured, adding layers of complexity to her character within the cosmic drama of the Godlike project.

Powers - Absolute Illusions:
Alice possesses the extraordinary ability to manipulate and control absolute illusions. Her mastery over illusions adds a captivating layer to her character, reflecting the intricacies of the cosmic forces at play in "Speak." These illusions, born from her experiences and emotions, shape her interactions within the narrative.

Unexpected Gesture:
Alice's arrival on the scene takes an unexpected turn when she steps onto the school bus and approaches Cyrus. Her act of offering companionship amidst the hostile environment of the bus sets the stage for a unique connection that defies the ordinary dynamics of the Godlike Agents.

Icy Resolve and Sternness:
Alice's demeanor is marked by an icy resolve and sternness that silences the school bus, leaving even the bullies, Tyrell and Miguel, apprehensive in her presence. Her character exudes a quiet strength, hinting at a background that has instilled in her the ability to face challenges head-on.

Understanding of Bullying:
Alice's intervention against the bullies reveals a keen understanding of the dynamics at play, suggesting that her past experiences may have acquainted her with the cruelty of bullying. Her response to the tormentors showcases a protective instinct that aligns with the underlying themes of power and protection in "Speak."

Curiosity and Friendship:

As Alice and Cyrus form an unlikely connection, her curiosity about Cyrus's passive response to bullying becomes a focal point. Their interactions unfold in a school setting, highlighting the contrast between the ordinary challenges faced by teenagers and the extraordinary cosmic struggles that define the Godlike Agents.

Mysterious Aura:

Throughout "Speak," Alice's mysterious aura adds an element of suspense, leaving readers intrigued about the illusions she can craft and how her past may intersect with the cosmic destinies of the Godlike project. Her character, though enigmatic, becomes a crucial piece in the celestial puzzle that unravels within the narrative.

MOROS NOCTIS

Character Bio: Moros Noctis - Cosmic Arbiter of Shadows

Background:
Moros Noctis emerges as a formidable force in the cosmic narrative of "Speak," embodying the essence of darkness and chaos. Conceived from Dr. Creed's desperation to avoid corruption, Moros Noctis becomes an intricate and malevolent entity, casting shadows over the Godlike Agents.

Unholy Fusion:
Moros Noctis is an unholy fusion of the once noble Peter Wayne, who held the grace of Uriel, and the corruptive nogitsune, a malevolent kitsune spirit residing within Dr. Creed. Fueled by the guilt of killing his best friend, Dr. Creed sought a desperate solution to contain the corruption.

Shadows of Corruption:
The nogitsune, a dark kitsune spirit, finds its dwelling within the lifeless vessel of Peter Wayne. This unholy union grants Moros Noctis dominion overshadows and the ability to manipulate the cosmic fabric, bringing forth a cosmic arbiter of darkness.

Cosmic Arbiter:
Moros Noctis becomes a cosmic arbiter, navigating the fine line between Dr. Creed's desire to prevent corruption and the unleashed darkness within. Its presence symbolizes the intricate dance between light and shadow, forcing the Godlike Agents to confront the consequences of their actions.

Malevolent Catalyst:
As the malevolent catalyst in "Speak," Moros Noctis shapes the narrative by introducing an intricate layer of moral ambiguity. Its creation raises questions about the lengths one is willing to go to prevent corruption, blurring the lines between savior and harbinger of chaos.

Conflict Within Darkness:
Moros Noctis harbors an internal conflict, balancing the remnants of Peter Wayne's nobility with the corruptive influence of the nogitsune. This duality adds depth to its character, transforming it into a cosmic entity grappling with the consequences of its own creation.

Shadow Manipulation:
Moros Noctis wields unparalleled power overshadows, manipulating them to weave cosmic chaos. Its abilities extend beyond physical manifestations, infiltrating the psyche of those it encounters and amplifying their fears, contributing to the overall cosmic struggle.

Legacy of Uriel
The grace of Uriel, once a divine force of light and guidance, lingers within Moros Noctis, serving as a haunting reminder of the noble intentions that paved the path to its creation. The legacy of Uriel becomes entwined with the darkness, creating a cosmic juxtaposition.

Ethereal Confrontation:
As Moros Noctis confronts the Godlike Agents, the ethereal clash becomes a pivotal point in the cosmic narrative. Its presence challenges the very essence of creation and destruction, forging a path that will redefine the fate of the universe.

Inescapable Shadows:
Moros Noctis's inescapable shadows cast a looming presence over the storyline, forcing characters to confront their own shadows and vulnerabilities. Its existence becomes a metaphorical representation of the inescapable consequences tied to the cosmic struggle within "Speak."

ETHAN

Character Bio: Ethan - The Phantom of Absolute Speed

Background:
Ethan, a pivotal character in "Speak," harnesses the extraordinary power of absolute speed, turning him into a phantom in the cosmic narrative. His presence is marked by rapid movements and an unparalleled swiftness that leaves others struggling to comprehend his actions.

Speed Unleashed:
Ethan's power grants him the ability to move at speeds beyond mortal comprehension. Whether weaving through dimensions or executing lightning-fast strikes in combat, he is the embodiment of velocity itself. The very air seems to ripple in his wake as he navigates the cosmic dance.

Time-Bending Agility:
Ethan's absolute speed extends beyond physical movement, allowing him a unique mastery over the manipulation of time. In moments of intense confrontation, he can bend time to his advantage, making him an elusive and formidable force in any cosmic struggle.

Phantom Presence:
Ethan's speed grants him a phantom-like quality, making it challenging for others to perceive his true form. He operates in the shadows, leaving behind only a blur of motion as evidence of his swift interventions.

Enigma in Motion:
Within the cosmic ballet of gods and godlike beings, Ethan remains an enigma, a phantom with absolute speed. His role in the unfolding narrative adds layers of complexity, keeping allies and adversaries alike on edge as they attempt to unravel the mysteries surrounding this speedster of cosmic proportions.

INUGAMI

Character Bio: Inugami - Mythical Guardian of Cyrus Finch

Origins:
The Inugami, a mythical creature of Japanese folklore, becomes a central figure in the cosmic struggles depicted in "Speak." This ethereal being is summoned by Cyrus Finch, serving as both guardian and weapon in the celestial conflicts.

Guardian Spirit:
The Inugami manifests as a supernatural dog, blending divine and mythical attributes. Its presence is both protective and formidable, embodying the ancient tales of loyal guardianship found in Japanese mythology.

Reality-Warping Powers:
Endowed with reality-warping abilities, the Inugami is a potent force on the cosmic battleground. Cyrus commands this mythical creature to unleash torrents of flames, whirlwinds, and other elemental forces, shaping reality itself in the pursuit of victory.

Sacrificial Empowerment:
A unique aspect of the Inugami's power lies in its connection to the sacrifices made by Cyrus's followers. Each command, each unleashed force, requires a sacrifice, fueling the Inugami's abilities with the life force of those devoted to Cyrus.

Symbol of Divine Inquisition:
In the narrative of "Speak," the Inugami transforms Cyrus's once-hallowed sanctum into an arena of divine inquisition. Its presence challenges the very core of Cyrus's god complex, becoming a symbol of both divine protection and the toll exacted in the pursuit of godlike power.

Celestial Companion:
As the story unfolds, the Inugami becomes more than a mythical weapon; it evolves into a celestial companion, intricately woven into the tapestry of the cosmic conflicts. Its loyalty to Cyrus and the sacrifices it demands contribute to the intricate dynamics of the godlike realm depicted in "Speak."

LILY

Character Bio: Lily - Bearer of God's Strength

Background:
Lily, a seemingly ordinary schoolgirl, emerges as an extraordinary figure in the cosmic battles of "Speak." Unbeknownst to her peers, she carries the divine essence of God's strength within her, making her a pivotal player in the unfolding celestial drama.

Divine Endowment:
Endowed with the strength of a deity, Lily's powers surpass the limits of mortal capabilities. Her physical strength becomes an embodiment of divine might, allowing her to wield unparalleled force in the conflicts that shape the godlike realm depicted in "Speak."

Unassuming Persona:
Lily's true nature remains hidden beneath the facade of a typical schoolgirl. Her unassuming appearance conceals the extraordinary power that lies within, adding an element of surprise to the unfolding narrative.

Catalyst for Change:
As the cosmic struggles intensify, Lily's divine strength becomes a catalyst for change. Her interactions with other godlike beings and the pivotal role she plays in the battles contribute to the evolving dynamics of power and conflict within the narrative.

Balancing Act:
In the godlike hierarchy depicted in "Speak," Lily's divine strength serves as a balancing force. Amidst the chaos and celestial clashes, she becomes a counterpoint to the godly entities, adding layers of complexity to the overarching themes of power and its consequences.

Symbol of Hidden Potential:
Lily's character embodies the idea that strength, both physical and divine, can often be concealed beneath the surface. Her journey in "Speak" explores the themes of hidden potential, unexpected heroes, and the transformative nature of power within the context of a godlike realm.